G

DATE DUE			3 / 02
JUL 3 0 02			
FEB 06 04 JUN 22 04			
10-15-19			
GAYLORD			PRINTED IN U.S.A.

Border Bandit

Border Bandit

RAY HOGAN

Sagebrush
Large Print Westerns

Library of Congress Cataloging-in-Publication Data

Hogan, Ray.
 Border bandit / Ray Hogan.
  p.   cm.
 ISBN 1-57490-386-1 (lg. print : hardcover)
 1. Large type books. I. Title

Due to recent problems with the mail, complete Library of
Congress Cataloging-in-Publication Data was not available at
the time of publication.

Libraries should call (800) 818-7574 and we will fax or mail
the CIP Data upon request.

Cataloging in Publication Data is available from
the British Library and the National Library of Australia.

Sagebrush Large Print Westerns are published in the United
States and Canada by Thomas T. Beeler, Publisher, PO Box 659,
Hampton Falls, New Hampshire 03844-0659. ISBN 1-57490-386-1

Published in the United Kingdom, Eire, and the Republic of
South Africa by Isis Publishing Ltd, 7 Centremead, Osney
Mead, Oxford OX2 0ES England. ISBN 0-7531-6682-3

Published in Australia and New Zealand by Bolinda Publishing
Pty Ltd, 17 Mohr Street, Tullamarine, Victoria, Australia, 3043
ISBN 1-74030-653-8

Manufactured by Sheridan Books in Chelsea, Michigan.

Border Bandit

PROLOGUE

HE WAS CALLED TOM SCHRADER, BUT HIS NAME COULD have been any one of many he had used during the forty-seven years of his life. So extensive in fact had been the variation—and with the passage of tumultuous time dulling the points of his own memory—it was likely that even he scarcely recalled the name with which his parents had christened him.

Now, as he looked ahead through the stacked layers of heat shimmering in the narrow depths of Skeleton Canyon, the clumps of yellow muscat and the gray-greens of oak and other wild growth were blurred colors in the shifting, dust-ridden atmosphere. Here and there phlox and red paintcup laid vivid splashes among the rocks and stunted trees, but on the whole it was a blending sameness, unfolding in a muted, desolate sort of beauty.

He raised his tough, gullied face and touched the soaring flight of a Mexican eagle high above the peaks of the Peloncillos with flat eyes. He and his companions had seen a lot of the huge, golden birds since they left the Chihuahua Desert, and somehow they filled Tom Schrader with a strange foreboding. The eagle circled and dipped, surged upward into the steel blue, then plunged. *Like a Goddamn buzzard,* he thought, *trailing us to hell.*

He should be feeling good, not worried about anything. They had pulled off the job at the Sabine Mine, deep in central Mexico, without a hitch. Riding behind him on his saddle was a healthy fortune in pure gold. His share would be enough to pleasure any

1

man. But for some obscure reason he was ill at ease.

Again he looked ahead. They were boring deeper into the Peloncillos, and the lonely route was becoming less assuring with each passing breath while the suffocating heat, seeping in from the desert to the south and the barren wastes of Arizona to the west, was rising steadily in intensity. He swore softly, deeply. He had not wanted to risk Skeleton Canyon; it was a haven for Mexican and American outlaws—and a favored hunting ground for the savage Chiricahua Apaches.

The trail through it was used regularly by smugglers up from Mexico who were headed for Tucson and points west, and any traveler found upon it was therefore looked upon as fair, possibly rich, pickings. But there had been no choice—thanks to those sonofabitching Mex guards who had tried to stop them at the Sabine. Crossing the Peloncillo Mountains into Arizona had been the only answer.

Schrader eased about on the saddle seeking to relax the aching muscles of his back. Brushing at the salty sweat clouding his eyes, he glanced at the five men strung out in single file behind him. Ike Bradley was immediately to his rear. Ike grinned wryly through the powdery dust and sweltering heat, and wagged his head.

Following Bradley was Dan Wyatt, his quiet face set to solemn lines. Wyatt hadn't liked the thought of Skeleton Canyon either. He was a good man and they had partnered for several years. He bore the appearance of a gambler, but he was such only in that he was willing to take a risk—any risk—if the stakes were high enough. If odds ever worried him, he did not reveal it. He was looking down now, chin resting on his chest, eyes squeezed to slits in an effort to minimize the glare.

Next came Hart Vickery. Schrader didn't care much

for him. He was short of twenty-five years of age but as deadly and tricky a man with a gun as ever walked a crowded street. He met Schrader's gaze unwaveringly—cool, defiant, vaguely hostile. Someday there would be trouble between them.

Trailing Hart was the kid—Chris Harper. He had fallen in with them back in Abilene less than a year ago. Schrader had taken him in on the Sabine Mine deal only because he had grown up in Mexico, knew the country, and talked the language like a native. The family, or at least his older brother, Poe, still ran a ranch along the east slopes of the Sierra Madres.

They had halted there overnight on their way back to the border. Poe had been a tough, right-down-the-middle sort of bucko who hadn't cottoned much to his brother's friends.

Bringing up the rear was Barney Johnson, his features drawn to their usual strained angles. Barney was a worrier, always expected the worst. He had been certain the robbery would foul up, but so far he had been wrong. He caught Schrader's glance, shook his head, blinked his narrow-set, hooded eyes, and spat. Barney still wasn't convinced.

"Sure be glad when we get through these mountains and hit Arizona." Bradley's voice was hoarse from the dust.

Vickery grunted. "Long ride to Tucson even after that."

"Maybe so, but it'll be out in the open. Half the country could be hidin' in this Goddamn brush."

"Likely is," Barney Johnson said. "Always somebody getting jumped along here."

Schrader grinned humorlessly and turned around. He heard Bradley say, "We splittin' up when we get there?"

3

And Wyatt's reply. "No cause. Be plenty miles between us and the Sabine Mine. We make a pretty fair team. Seems we ought to hold together. Money'll run out soon."

"It'll take a spell. We got three, four thousand dollars apiece."

"Women and liquor come high in Tucson. Won't last long as you think."

"That what you're doing with your share, kid?" Hart Vickery asked.

"Won't be much thrown away on whiskey," Harper replied. "Women—well, that's something else."

Vickery snorted. "I'm betting you'll play out before the money does."

"Maybe so, but I'm sure aching to give it a try."

He'll learn, Tom Schrader thought. Man could blow a thousand a night on whorehouses, saloons, and the faro tables without half trying. But so what? That was what money was for. What pleasure did a man get out of money if he didn't spend it?

Oh, sure, he could settle down, like Poe Harper, build himself a ranch, someday amount to something, if you did your calculating along those lines. But who wanted to spend his life nursing a bunch of stinking cows? Anyway, it was too late for that where he was concerned. It had been too late for twenty-five years— ever since he had put a bullet in that hick-town marshal back in Missouri. Besides, it was easier this way, and a man got more kick out of it.

Schrader reached back and laid his hand on the black, heavily scrolled saddlebags draped behind the cantle of his saddle. He allowed his fingers to caress the bulging pouches. How long would it take a man to come up with twenty thousand dollars or so in pure gold raising cows?

4

It had cost them less than an hour's time—not counting the coming and going. How long would a rancher slave to make that kind of money? A lifetime, he reckoned.

He frowned, his eyes on a ledge of rock a hundred yards ahead on the twisting, tortured trail. Something had moved. He had had only a fleeting glimpse of motion, and that was all. A bird, he decided after a moment. Or it could had been one of the small, striped chipmunks that populated the rocks.

"Tom . . ."

He became aware of Barney Johnson's voice. He brushed at the sweat on his face again, tugged at his short collar, and turned half about. "Yeah?"

"You figure there's anything to them yarns about gold coming from that Sabine mine being cursed? You know what I mean . . ."

"Sure I know. Heard those tales plenty, but far's I'm concerned, gold's gold. To my way of thinking, the curse comes from not having any."

Ike Bradley laughed. "Cursed or not, I'm sure lookin' forward to spendin' my share. God—just thinkin' about all them women, all gussied up and smellin' of perfume . . . And waitin' . . ."

Johnson, still serious, said, "How far we from Tucson? How long will it take us to get there?"

"Four days—if we're lucky," Schrader answered and settled back.

"Four days!" Barney echoed in a falling voice. "I ain't sure—"

The sharp, dry slap of a rifle shot crashed through the withering heat, went rushing off into the hushed side canyons and up to the silent ridges and peaks.

Tom Schrader felt the solid shock of a bullet as it drove into his chest and knocked him half off the

5

saddle. He started to fall but seized the horn. He caught a glimpse of a dark, paint-daubed face, a head of coarse, black hair. It bobbed up in the rocks beyond a ledge, then disappeared instantly.

"Apaches!" he yelled through the clawing pain in his breast. "Get in the brush!"

He heard the others wheel into the shelter of the shrubbery, yelling and cursing at their worn horses as they slid and clattered over the rocky soil. He spun his bay about and plunged after them, having difficulty staying in the stirrups. More rifle shots blasted through the confusion. The drone of passing bullets became a high sing-song around his head.

He winced as a second slug seared into his body. *Right in the belly,* he thought, and swore deeply. But he wasn't too sure. He was still numb from the first bullet. He wheeled in beside the others, off their horses and crouched, trying to locate the hidden Apaches. Schrader slid awkwardly from the saddle and went to his knees. He caught the horn in one hand, cantle in the other, and hung there. It was like having no legs—nothing from the hips down.

"Tom's hit!"

He nodded woodenly at Vickery's shout. Wyatt rushed up and caught him under the arms.

"The gold!" Schrader gasped, finding it an effort to speak. "Grab it—bury it. Don't want them Goddamn guteaters getting it . . ."

"He's right," Wyatt yelled. "Barney—get the saddlebags, hide them under that log. Case any of us comes out of this, we can drop back—pick them up."

"If we come out of it," Johnson grumbled, his fingers struggling with the leather strings that held the pouches to the saddle.

Tom Schrader heard them speaking as if from a distance. He felt Wyatt pull him away from the bay and lay him out full length on the trash-littered floor of the arroyo into which they had turned. Angrily, he shook off Wyatt's hands and fought himself to a sitting position.

"My rifle—Goddammit, give me my rifle!" he muttered. "They'll be hitting us again in a couple of minutes. We got to be ready."

ONE

WHEN THE FIRST BULGE OF YELLOW DUST APPEARED on the horizon to the south, Poe Harper rose from the table where he had been going over his accounts, strapped on his .45, and stepped out onto the shaded portico of the house.

The blistering heat from the mighty Chihuahua Desert struck him head-on as he emerged from the sanctuary of the cool, adobe-walled structure, and he flinched involuntarily. He grinned. What the hell? He'd lived on the edge of the desert almost all his life—you'd think he'd be getting used to it by now.

He walked to the edge of the shadow, his dark eyes on the boil of dust, brow furrowed into deep creases. It could be bandits again. They hadn't been around for several months. It was about time for another raid. Usually they accomplished nothing more than an interruption of work on Muleshoe, since old Jed Harper had done a good job of fortifying the ranch for just such emergencies. But every now and then, it seemed, they had to make their try.

He studied the cloud for a time, a tall, dark-haired, dark-eyed man in his mid-twenties, with a hard, bony face too angular to be handsome. He reached for the iron bar, briefly considered hammering out the usual warning on the metal triangle hanging at the end of the porch, then decided to wait out a few more moments. Perhaps it was more unexpected visitors—as had been Chris and his friends that previous day.

Chris and five men had ridden in around dark and asked to be put up for the night. His brother had said they were heading for San Luis Pass, then striking west for Tucson—possibly on to California.

"Still could be a little gold left in the hills there," the one named Wyatt had remarked with a grin.

They had been doing a little prospecting down to the south, he had continued but with no luck. Poe had doubted the man; their hands were too soft, and they didn't have that hard-scrabbled look of prospectors. But they were his brother's friends, and he made no issue of it. He had tried to talk Chris into staying on at the ranch. In reality it belonged to both of them, an inheritance from their father, but Chris had not been interested.

He never had. He had changed little from the way he was when he chucked his share and rode out almost two years ago—restless, unsettled, and never happy with hard work and the thought of tying himself down. He was like his father in that respect. He even looked like Jed Harper—red hair, ruddy face, lantern jaw, with a smiling way to him that made friends easily. Poe, it seemed, took after his dark-eyed mother.

But there was a broad difference between Jed and his son Chris in other ways. Jed had been a man of vision and drive—one who worked hard and played hard. And the fine ranch he handed down to his two sons was a worthy monument to his industry and foresight. It was a shame Chris couldn't be like him in that respect too. Chris always took the easy way; he was lazy, footloose—well, why not tag it right? He was a shiftless no-account, and about as much use around Muleshoe as teats on a boar hog.

And there was the woman problem. He was always after the young daughters of the peons. He had put several of them in a family way—and God only knew how many of the wives he had got to. It had become so

9

bad that if it hadn't been for Rojo Peralta, Muleshoe's half-Yaqui, half-Spanish foreman, Chris likely would have ended up on the brushy slopes of the Sierra Madres with a knife in his back.

But Rojo had managed to smooth matters over, although toward the last things had got a bit touchy. No, it was just as well Chris didn't return to the ranch. He was a born drifter, and he was better off in the company of men such as Schrader and Wyatt and the like. They were of the same stripe and understood him.

The dust roll grew larger, lifting higher above the plain, which was dotted with creosote bushes and cactus. A fair-sized party of riders, Poe guessed, too large for casual visitors. He raised the length of iron and rang the triangle sharply three times. All *vaqueros* and field hands within hearing distance would immediately abandon their work, take up weapons, and move to positions about the ranch previously assigned them by Peralta. They would be waiting and ready when the bandits arrived.

Poe owed a lot to Peralta, who, oddly enough, had the same red hair and florid complexion as Chris—and Jed—Harper. He was a good *segundo,* knew how to handle the *vaqueros* and the other Mexicans, get the best out of them with a minimum of friction.

Thanks to the Yaqui, it would be a fine year for Muleshoe—one that would pay off handsomely. Poe had over fifteen hundred prime steers ready for market, and a good stand of feed and garden produce. The San Pedro river, though no credit to Rojo, of course, had not petered out in midsummer as it generally did, and there had been no shortage of water. But the Yaqui had known how to make the most of that unexpected gift of nature.

Finally, he would be able to do all the things he had struggled for so long to accomplish; for one thing, he could buy some new breeding stock—both bulls and stallions. And the ranch needed a new barn, improvements on the main house, better furniture, larger quarters for the hired help. But most of all, he and Edwina could now get married.

Thinking of Ed McGarrity's daughter sent a warm glow through him. He had first met her three years ago, not long after he had returned from doing his bit with Hood's Texas Brigade. He had ridden up to the McGarrity ranch, just across the border in the Aimas Valley of New Mexico, to see about selling some of his cattle.

Edwina—slender, dark haired, blue eyed, and with a face that could be angelic or devilish, whichever suited her mood at any particular moment—had captured his fancy immediately. The friendship had grown, but he had resisted the idea of marriage consistently. It was not because he opposed any thoughts of a union; in fact, he hungered for her constantly. It was simply that he refused to bring her into a life he felt was not on a level with that she enjoyed under her father's roof.

Edwina insisted that it mattered not, and to her he knew it didn't. But Poe Harper could be stubborn. He would deny himself the one thing he wanted most until he could provide properly—and that was the way it had hung for well over two years. Now the end was in sight; he could marry Edwina and give her a home every bit as good as Ed McGarrity's.

The quick drum of a running horse brought Poe half around. He glanced up and saw Peralta. Inside the house he could hear old Carmelita rattling her pans and dishes as she prepared for the evening meal. Like Rojo, the wrinkled, ancient woman had been on Muleshoe since its inception, one of the original hands with whom Jed Harper had built the ranch.

The Yaqui wheeled into the yard, his solemn face expressionless, and drew up at the hitchrack. He dropped lightly from his ornate Mexican saddle, wrapped the reins about the pole, then paused to glance at the dust. He was only a few years older than Poe— five or six—Poe never could remember, and looking at him there, profiled, Harper had the thought that had occurred to him many times in the past.

Peralta's mother had been a Yaqui Indian woman; his father, it was said, had been a red-haired Spaniard. It was possible, of course, but occasionally Poe had the uncomfortable feeling that there were things about Rojo's ancestry he did not understand. But as before, he brushed all speculation aside; what Jed Harper did during the years in which he knocked about Mexico before marrying was Jed's business.

The Yaqui brushed his silver-trimmed *sombrero* to the back of his head and waved at the dust. "Many riders. It is such that disturbs you?"

"Could be *bandidos*. Haven't had them on our necks for quite a spell. The men ready?"

Peralta moved in under the shade of the porch. He nodded and leaned back against the wall. "They are ready." He frowned, studying the dust. "There has been no word of *bandidos*."

"Know that, but they could have sneaked in this time. From the size of that cloud there's one hell of a bunch of them. Right now we could use the Federales."

The Yaqui grunted and turned his head to one side. "*Federales—boñiga de caballo,*" he said, and spat. "We are better off with the women and children."

12

Poe grinned. To Rojo the Mexican army was of no value at all. It could never be found when needed; yet the *cantinas* in the larger towns overflowed with uniformed men. But even the specially trained and equipped Rurales were seldom seen in that part of the Chihuahua Desert area.

Peralta glanced toward the door. "Chris—he has gone?"

"Pulled out a couple of hours before dawn. Couldn't get him to stay."

Relief was immediate and apparent on the Yaqui's features. "It is best, *compañero,*" he said, employing the affectionate term he had applied to Poe since they were small boys together. "He is restless, that one. For Tucson?"

"For Tucson, and maybe on to California. They said they were looking for gold."

The Yaqui shrugged. His face took on the blank, unrevealing aspect typical of his Indian heritage. "It is not in the hills they search for gold. It is in other places."

"Just what I figured, but it was none of my business. Chris will do what he pleases—and to hell with everybody else. I'm just hoping he doesn't get himself in bad trouble."

"To him trouble will come. Your hope is like the mirage."

Poe did not reply, his gaze again on the now close roll of dust. Rojo was right, he knew; but Chris was his brother, and he had little left but hope where Chris was concerned. Their mother had died when Chris was born. Jed had followed her ten years later, leaving the upbringing of Chris to him and the ranch hands.

He had done his best, but Chris was the sort who

always followed his own inclinations and Poe had suspected he wasn't doing a very good job of it. When Chris shucked his share in Muleshoe and moved on, he knew it was true. Still, there was nothing he could do about it; Chris was a grown man, able to think for himself.

"These riders come near," Rojo observed, squinting into the brilliant sunlight. "Perhaps it is well that I see to the men."

Harper studied the yellowish cloud. "Only one thing bothers me," he murmured, half-aloud. "*Bandidos* coming in from the desert—doesn't make sense. Always before they've moved in from the mountains, figuring to get in close before we spotted them. We've seen this bunch for miles—and they know it."

"It is so, but who else would come in so large a party? It moves too fast for cattle being driven. If you say, I will ride forth and look—"

"No need," Poe broke in, turning away from the dazzling glare. "Just caught a glimpse of a uniform. It's the Federales."

"Federales!" the Yaqui echoed, surprised. "For what reason would they come here?"

Poe Harper shrugged. "Who knows? But I reckon they're better than *bandidos*. Signal the men back to work."

TWO

HARPER WATCHED THE YOUNG CAPTAIN AND HIS TWENTY or so surly-faced soldiers ride into the yard. This was no ordinary patrol duty—they were too far north for that. And never before had the Mexican Government taken

14

any interest in the wild, sparsely settled country lying along the Sierra Madres. No, they had come for some specific reason; there was something wrong.

The officer, a lean, tough-looking, black-eyed man with a thin mustache, pulled to the hitchrack and halted. Sweat lay in glistening patches on his skin, and dust had dulled the glittering gold braid, mottled the cornflower blue of his well-tailored uniform. A career man, Poe guessed; son of some wealthy family, out to make a name for himself in military circles.

For several moments the officer considered Poe with arrogant detachment; then, shifting the position of his saber, he spoke.

"*Buenos tardes*. This is the ranch called Muleshoe? You are Poe Harper?"

Poe nodded, irritated by the officer's supercilious manner. Put a uniform on some of these roosters and they think they're God almighty himself.

"Right," he said curtly. "What can I do for you?"

Somewhere back in the restless ranks of the soldiers a man laughed and muttered something. Others laughed. Anger swept through Poe Harper.

"You are the owner of this ranch?" the captain continued as though making doubly certain of the person to whom he was speaking.

"I am!" Harper snapped. "Been here all my life."

The officer nodded. "I am Captain Luis Salcedo, from Chihuahua City," he said with correct stiffness. "My men and I have ridden a very long road."

"No doubt," Poe said with disinterest. He had been wrong; the Federales wanted only a place to get in out of the hot sun, rest, and water their horses. He preferred not having them around at all; it usually led to trouble, but you didn't turn a man away—not with the

15

Chihuahua Desert at his back. "If you want to stop over for a bit, you're welcome," he said grudgingly.

Salcedo did not stir. "It is a matter of much more importance that brings me."

One of the horses shied suddenly, thudding hard against the animal next him. A thick-shouldered sergeant at the captain's left rose in his stirrups and bawled a heated reprimand at the offending cavalryman. "I did nothing," the soldier protested. "There are flies. Huge fellows. They are like wolves . . ."

Harper scarcely heard. He was eyeing the captain, endeavoring to fathom his words. He hadn't been wrong after all. "Important to me—or to you?"

"To both, I fear."

Poe glanced at Peralta. The *segundo* was watching with narrow, suspicion-filled attention, one hand on the pistol at his hip. The Yaqui's dislike for army men was so pronounced that the smallest thing could set him off, create an incident. Harper frowned, shook his head slightly, then swung back to Salcedo.

"Maybe you'd better step down, Captain, tell me what this is all about."

The officer came off the saddle and stalked stiffly into the shade of the porch. His sergeant, still mounted, edged in closer as though desiring to be near his superior in event his presence became necessary. Inside the house Carmelita continued to rattle pans and crockery, and down near the corrals one of the pack burros used for hauling wood from the hills brayed noisily.

Salcedo removed his plumed shako. It's tight inner band left a crimson mark across his forehead, and his crown of dark, curly hair was plastered tight to his skull with sweat. The officer was unbending; however, he

16

maintained his absolute military decorum and betrayed no signs of discomfort.

"You have heard of the Sabine Mine señor Harper?"

A small sound exploded in Rojo Peralta's throat. *"Oro del maldito,"* he muttered, staring at Poe.

Poe shrugged. The Sabine—who hadn't? The richest gold mine in the country, situated in the Ocampo district. Rumored to be secretly owned and operated by the government or a combine of high officials, it was famed for two things—the purity of its product and the so-called curse that attended it.

The deep shafts were worked by slave labor, many of the workers being political prisoners. Once there, a man remained until death released him. Drops of blood slashed from straining bodies by the merciless whips of brutal guards, and mixing with the ore, brought about the curse of the Sabineros, it was said. Any person thereafter coming in contact with the gold was doomed to eternal damnation and misfortune.

"Heard of it," Harper said. "What's it got to do with me?"

"You have heard also perhaps that there was a robbery, that not only was twenty thousand dollars in gold taken, but four trusted guards were slain?"

Poe stirred. "Hadn't heard that. When did it happen?"

"Three days ago. Did you not see the bandits pass this way? Were they not here going to the border?"

Harper shook his head. "Been no bandits by here that I know of."

The thick-shouldered sergeant impatiently shifted in the driving heat. *"Palabra de gringo—nada! Despreciable!"* he spat.

Word of an Anglo—nothing! Worthless.

Anger surged through Poe Harper in a sudden blast.

17

He came off the porch in three long strides. His hand shot out. His fingers wrapped about the sergeant's arm. With a powerful heave, he hauled the man from the saddle. The sergeant yelled, recovered his balance, and whirled. Harper's fist smashed into his jaw and sent him down under his nervously dancing horse. A shout went up from the soldiers.

"Hold!" Salcedo's barked command brought instant silence.

Poe, legs spraddled, arms hanging at his sides, glared at the sergeant, who was now crawling hurriedly beyond range of the horse's sharp hooves. He stood up, face flushed, eyes blazing. He took a half step toward Harper.

"Sergeant Nuanes!" Salcedo roared. "You will come to attention!"

The squat noncom stiffened. The Mexican officer swept him with a cold look. "You will watch your tongue, Sergeant. Now get back on your horse!"

The soldier saluted, spun, and went back to the saddle. Poe, sweat streaming from every pore in his body, returned to the shade of the porch. Salcedo watched him thoughtfully.

"It was said to me, señor, that you are one of great violence, of harsh temper. This I can see is true."

"Nobody calls me a liar," Harper snarled, still simmering. "Especially a two-bit soldier."

The corners of the officer's mouth tightened. There was no apology in his tone when he said, "Perhaps Sergeant Nuanes was right."

Anger again flared through Harper. "Goddammit, Salcedo, you want trouble too? Just because you're wearing all that braid and toting a saber doesn't mean a thing to me. I said there'd been no bandits here—and I meant it!"

18

"You tell me that six men did not come this way yesterday?" the Federale asked calmly. "That you did not give them food and shelter for the night—and that they did not ride from here for the border this morning?"

With a shock Poe realized Salcedo was referring to Chris and his friends. He had given them no thought, but apparently the Mexican captain and his troopers had been trailing them—a day behind. Loyal countrymen, and the Rurales, evidently had kept him well posted enroute.

He felt a sinking in his belly when understanding came to him; that was the prospecting for gold Wyatt had mentioned—robbing the Sabine Mine. It was hard to believe that his brother could be mixed up in something as serious as robbery and murder—but it could be true. Chris, much younger than the other men, had been right under their thumbs.

But that was the army's problem, not his. He had long since washed his hands of Chris. He nodded. "Sure, they were here. I fed them and let them stay, but I sure as hell didn't know they'd robbed a mine or killed anybody. If I had, it still wouldn't have been any of my business."

Salcedo's expression revealed nothing. He simply waited.

"They rode out early this morning," Poe continued. "Around four o'clock. You push on you can likely overtake them."

"It is possible," the officer said quietly. "Only it cannot be done by me."

"Why not?"

"There is a treaty between our governments. It will not permit me to lead soldiers across the border. This

19

you know. I cannot pursue these men beyond the line."

"You can get permission. All you have to do is tell your government to get in touch with the American—"

"Such would mean much delay," Salcedo interrupted curtly. "Regrettably, there is always much politics involved in these matters. And meanwhile these bandits—these killers of honest men—would escape and become lost for all time."

A hard core of suspicion was growing within Poe Harper. He studied Salcedo's swarthy face. "Not necessarily," he said after a few moments. "Notify the authorities across the border to be on the watch for a party of six men—if you're dead sure they're the ones you want."

"They are the ones, of that be assured," the captain murmured. "As to the authorities, there is not time to return to Chihuahua City and make such a request. It is important that what is to be done is done immediately."

"You're wasting time then," Harper said abruptly. "You'll not catch them hanging around here."

"A truth, but this you can—and will—do for me."

There was little surprise in Poe Harper's angry eyes. He had figured Salcedo was leading up to that point.

"No, thanks," he snapped. "I make it a policy to keep out of other people's business—particularly the army's. I've got problems of my own without inviting more."

"But it is your problem, señor. I make it so."

"The hell you do!" Harper shouted. "Just because you bungled your job and let those outlaws slip through your fingers, don't think you can come riding in here and order me to bail you out! It's your worry, not mine."

Rojo Peralta, slouched against the wall, silent through

it all, drew himself up slowly. Salcedo glanced at him, then allowed his eyes to sweep his soldiers briefly. Finally, he came back to Poe.

"I think, perhaps, it is your worry, *amigo*. One of the bandits is your brother. This I know."

THREE

IN THE HOT STILLNESS THAT FOLLOWED LUIS SALCEDO'S remarks, the only sound was the clicking of insects in the heat-blasted weeds. Harper, restraining his temper with effort, lifted his shoulders, then permitted them to sag.

"So my brother is one of them. What's that got to do with me?"

"A very great deal," the officer said. "To you he will not offer resistance. He will likely persuade the others to surrender and not fight you. Were I involved there would be guns used and blood would be spilled. This I would avoid."

Salcedo was fooling no one. Poe gave him a stiff, sneering smile. "What's the difference? You said there were four men killed in the robbery. Don't you think I know what will happen to my brother and the others if they give themselves up?"

The captain nodded. "It would be a matter for the courts to decide."

"And we both know the answer to that—hanging or a firing squad. Forget it, Captain. I'll have nothing to do with it."

The Federale officer sighed. He walked to the end of the portico slowly and looked off toward the corrals, the barns and lesser buildings. Beyond them lay the fields

21

standing deep and lush with hay and ripening grain. Old Carmelita's garden was a vivid green square of chili plants, tomatoes, and other vegetables. And farther spread the long slopes red-carpeted with owl clover. He could see none of the cattle, for the herds were scattered, grazing in a dozen different sections of the range.

"It is a very fine ranch," he said in a low voice. "A pity should it be lost to you after so much hard labor."

Rojo Peralta's face darkened. His shoulders came back. "For a long time it is the property of the Harpers. It shall remain so!" he said fiercely.

Salcedo turned lazily, allowing his gaze to settle on the Yaqui. "So. The mestizo has a sharp tongue."

At the loathed term Peralta's eyes flashed. He moved forward, quick and smooth as a gliding snake. Poe flung out his arm hastily, checked him, pressed him back gently.

"You're talking to me, Captain," he said coldly. "If you want to throw around insults, try throwing them at me."

Salcedo smiled faintly. "It is a matter of truth."

"Has nothing to do with you and me. What you just said—do I take that as a threat?"

"That also is a matter of truth. You must take it as you see fit."

Poe Harper was accustomed to the polite, roundabout way the Spanish had of arriving at a point, but he was suddenly growing weary of it.

"This was my father's ranch before it was mine—a gift from your government to him," he said. "That gift has always been honored by your presidents and the governors of Chihuahua."

"There is no record—no deed," Salcedo murmured

22

with a wave of his hand. "There is only the word that such a gift was made."

"Still a fact. I expect you can find a few men around the palace who will remember it."

I hope, Poe thought, as a new sort of fear began to creep through him. It had happened a long time back— and politics and the men who guide the destiny of a restless country change rapidly.

There had been no proper transaction conveying, officially, the land to Jed Harper. It had come about shortly after the close of the war between the United States and Mexico. Jed had been in the Sierra Madres prospecting when the trouble broke out. He had remained neutral—although sympathetic with Mexico and its problems, he had been unwilling to fight against his homeland.

Later, when the Peace of Guadalupe Hidalgo came in 1848, he had volunteered his services in an advisory capacity to the Mexican Government. The President had been grateful and had rewarded Jed with his choice of land upon which he could build himself a ranch.

Harper, already well acquainted with northern Chihuahua state and the country along the Sierra Madres, asked for a grant of land in that area. He was given one hundred square miles lying in the gap of the Y formed by the San Pedro and Casas Grandes rivers.

Jed, having a way with land, had immediately set to work building himself an empire. When it was well on its way he returned to Texas, married the girl who was waiting for him, and brought her to his new domain. Later Poe, and then Chris, were born—both in Texas; Elizabeth Harper was determined her sons would not be born on foreign soil.

Thus the Muleshoe holdings were founded. Down

through the years succeeding governors and lesser politicians had honored the grant made to Jed Harper, and while there was always talk of making the gift official, nothing was ever done about it.

Jed had made two or three attempts to obtain a written deed conveying title to him, and once, while in Chihuahua City, Poe had looked into the matter. As before there were promises but no real effort on the part of officials to get things settled. Maximilian had been deposed, officialdom was in a state of flux, and it was impossible to accomplish anything.

And so the situation had rocked on—an understanding rather than a fact. Poe, his throat dry, felt the grip of real fear. He blamed himself bitterly; he should have hung himself around the politicians' necks and stayed right with the problem until he had settled it properly.

Salcedo drew a slender black cigar from his pocket. "Regardless, you must understand that you are here by courtesy of my government. Such is fact."

"I doubt if your government has so short a memory as that," Poe replied brusquely. His confidence was more sham than actual, but it would be a mistake to reveal that. "My father worked hard in the interests of Mexico, then worked just as hard to carve this ranch out of the desert. I don't think your government will overlook that, even if there is no written record of the transaction."

Salcedo lit his cigar, took a deep draught, and exhaled. He studied the cloud of blue smoke thoughtfully. "Such was a long time ago, señor. The face of politics changes."

"But not the honor of a country."

The Federale stiffened perceptibly—the Spanish were always touchy on the matter of honor—but he was equal to the moment. "Honor is a matter of—of perspective," he said.

Harper laughed. "You split hairs, Captain. Anyway, there may be a deed on record now. I was promised it would be done."

"It is not on record. The Governor of Chihuahua has advised me of that."

Poe frowned, uncertainty again grasping him. He had thought the whole thing had possibly been cooked up by Salcedo. It sounded otherwise. "The Governor in on this, too?"

"It is so. There have been too many criminals from your country inside our borders. He is determined to bring an end to this violation. These six, for the crime they have committed, are to become a warning, an example to others who believe they can with impunity enter our land and do as they wish."

"And I'm to be the goat who brings it all about."

Salcedo permited himself a smile. "You are the goat, señor."

Several cavalrymen laughed. The officer shot them a stern look. They silenced immediately.

"It is a matter of simplicity," the officer said, staring at the tip of his cigar. "You will go after your brother and his friends. You will return them and the stolen gold to me—here at this ranch. I have the word of the Governor to you that he personally will then see that there no longer exists any question of your title to this land, once it is done."

Anger was a steady current flowing through Poe Harper. It was high-level blackmail, and he could think of no greater pleasure in that moment then to reach out, grasp Luis Salcedo's neck with his fingers, and choke the arrogant, supercilious little bastard to death. The look on Rojo Peralta's face indicated that such was what he hoped for and expected—but Harper knew that it would accomplish nothing except a gratification of his own frustration. He had no one to blame but himself; he should have got that deed.

"And if I don't?" he pressed, determined to force the officer to state it clearly.

Salcedo hung one hand upon the hilt of his saber. "It will be necessary to confiscate this fine ranch in the name of my government. It will be of use as a military post. I shall recommend it as such."

"The hell you say!" Poe exploded, unable to hold back further. "You or nobody else is taking my land—"

"It is no longer yours, unless the obligation is fulfilled. All will become the property of the state—and you an unwelcome person within our borders."

A red mist swam before Poe Harper's eyes. Goddamn the lousy government! Goddamn Chris and those sons of bitches with him! Everything lost—down the river, just like that! All he had worked for, built up to . . . All Jed Harper had accomplished . . . And Edwina—that would end too. He could forget marrying her, starting the life he had planned. He would have nothing left—a flat nothing.

He glared at Salcedo, temper setting the corners of his mouth to quivering. From the tail of his eye he could see Rojo Peralta half-crouched as though ready to spring. They would have to kill the Yaqui before they took over; he would never give in. But such would go for nothing. It was hopeless to fight it.

"So that's the way it is," he said in a strained voice.

The officer nodded. "I bring you the word of the Governor. That is the way it *must* be."

"Unless I find my brother and the men with him,

bring them and that damned gold back to you—I lose everything. Boils down to that."

"It is so."

Poe felt Peralta's fingers clutch at his arm, heard him murmur, "You cannot do this, *compañero*. It is your brother. It is Chris you will kill . . ."

"The hell with Chris!" Poe shouted in exasperation. "I don't owe him a Goddamn thing! I tried to do right by him, but all I ever got back was the short end of the stick. He made his choice—he's the one who picked that bunch of outlaw bastards to run with—not me. Now let him pay up for it."

"But he is your own blood. There are other ways, perhaps, to fight . . . "

"Fight the whole Mexican Government when I don't have a leg to stand on? Hell, I'm licked before I start!"

"You would send him to death?"

"What do you think's going to happen to him sooner or later anyway? Somebody'll put a bullet through him while he's pulling a holdup or something. Doesn't make sense I should have to give up everything I've sweated for just to save him for that!"

His angry glance shifted to Salcedo, then swept to Nuanes and the stolid faces of the soldiers beyond as he tried to read their thoughts. He learned nothing. He stirred uneasily. Was he taking the wrong atitude? Chris was no good—still, they were of the same blood. But should that matter? After all, right was right, just as wrong was wrong, and Chris—Goddamn him—certainly was in the wrong.

A soberness came over Poe Harper. Maybe the alleged Sabine curse was already working—forcing him to think and say and do the wrong things . . . Maybe, but he doubted it. He didn't put much stock in curses and

27

witches and black cats. Such stuff was just so much horse manure. He brushed the doubt away.

"All right, Salcedo, you've made a deal. I'll go after them. Peralta and I'll pull out in the morning."

The captain nodded slowly. "It is wise. From this moment you have fifteen days in which to return."

FOUR

SALCEDO'S DARK EYES GLOWED EXULTANTLY. HARPER swore under his breath. The Federale had him by the short hair and knew it. But there was no other answer; he wasn't about to sacrifice two lifetimes of work, along with all his hopes, for a bunch of stinking outlaws. And that's what it amounted to—brother or not. They were outlaws, killers, and each knew he was taking his chances when he strapped on a gun and embarked on that way of life.

He wheeled to Peralta. "We leave early—about four in the morning. Get a couple of good horses ready. We'll need blanket rolls, ponchos—everything for the trail. Have Carmelita throw some grub in a sack."

Rojo looked down at his boots. "This is not good, *compañero*. You seek your brother for death—and it is the gold of the Sabine. Accursed gold, red with blood."

"Forget it!" Poe snapped. "We're going after them."

The Yaqui lifted his face and stared at Harper. His lips tightened. "You wish only that I go? There is no need for others?"

"Just the two of us. We go riding out of here with a posse, we'll not get within miles of them."

Peralta made no reply; he simply wheeled and entered the house.

28

Luis Salcedo removed the cigar from his mouth and held it poised. "If I might suggest, señor. Would it not be wise to leave now? The men you wish to catch can travel far between this hour and the time you plan to depart in the morning."

"They'll stop when it's dark," Poe said gruffly. "Horses they're riding were pretty well beat. Anyway, I can't leave now. Few things I've got to arrange before pulling out. This is a big ranch. Won't run itself."

"Such you can safely leave in my hands," the captain said. "I shall see that all goes well in your absence. Also, you will have the added protection of my men from *bandidos*."

"I fear the bandits less than I do the trouble your soldiers will stir up!" Harper snapped. "Keep them away from my people, Captain."

Salcedo's jaw hardened. Harper stalked to the edge of the porch and pointed to a long adobe structure beyond the corrals. "That bunkhouse is empty. Quarter your men there."

"And I?"

Harper gave the officer a cold glance. "There is room for you there too. However, if you insist, you can bunk here in the main house. I'll tell the cook to serve you at my table."

"My thanks," Salcedo said, bowing slightly. "It is always much better for discipline if an officer does not mingle with his men."

He spun on his boot heel and faced the still mounted cavalrymen. "Sergeant Nuanes! Garrison the men in the bunkhouse back of the corrals. We shall remain here for two weeks, perhaps less. My headquarters will be in this building. See to it that all is attended to, and then report to me."

Nuanes saluted and barked an order to the troopers. They cut around and cantered toward the far side of the yard. When they reached the corrals and were dismounting, their voices floated back, loud in conversation and laughter. Poe turned to the officer.

"Salcedo, I'm holding you personally responsible for the conduct of your men while they are here. They're guests. I want them to remember that."

"They are representatives of the Mexican Government," the Federale corrected in a stiff tone.

"Then see that they act as such—and don't get the idea they're a bunch of conquering heroes! If I hear of just one of my people—man or woman—being mistreated, you'll answer to me!"

Salcedo met Harper's burning stare squarely. "Let us hope, señor, that within two weeks you will be back and in a position of such authority as to fulfill that warning."

"I'll be here, Captain," Poe promised quietly. "Figure on it."

FIVE

A COLD WIND BRUSHED THE ROUGH, RAGGED BREAST of the Chihuahua Desert, not hard, scarcely strong enough to stir the dust into small spirals, but sufficient to make itself felt in the early-morning hours.

Poe Harper, astride the barrel-chested bay Peralta had chosen for him, pulled his jacket closer about his body and stared into the moon-silvered darkness. Gaunt, many-fingered chollas silhouetted against the night met his gaze, and off to the left, in the low hills bubbling about the foot of the towering Sierra Madres, coyotes had set up a raucous serenade.

The stars were out, giving wide support to the moon, and looking to the east Poe could see the peaks and ridges of the mountains along which the Santa Maria flowed. They had made good time, he realized, and shortly they would come to the ford that crossed the San Pedro. Peralta had picked for him a horse with bottom—one for staying power rather than speed. The bay, and the black Rojo himself rode, moved at a tireless lope.

A thought crossed Poe Harper's mind at that point— maybe he should have taken Salcedo's advice and set out after Chris and his outlaw friends earlier. At the pace the horses were moving they might have overtaken the party by dawn. He shrugged it off. It didn't matter. They would catch up—and it sure as hell wouldn't take any two weeks to get the job done.

He wondered what the Federale Commandante had been thinking of when he stated so generous a time limit. It was for his own benefit, and could be sure. Luis Salcedo was a cool customer and would do nothing without forethought. There was no doubt that he was out to save his own hide after allowing the outlaws to slip through his fingers.

He had played it smart. He knew there wasn't time enough to get permission from the United States Government to breach the border with troops, so he had done the next-best thing—put pressure where it would do the most good.

Was it all Salcedo's idea, or did he really have the backing of the Chihuahua politicians in his threat to appropriate Muleshoe? Poe had pondered that question earlier, realizing at the same time it was one to which he could find no quick answer. The Governor's palace was a long four-hundred-mile round trip from the ranch, and the only way he could determine for sure was to make the journey.

It was not worth the gamble, he had decided. If the Governor had issued the order, as Salcedo claimed, it would have then been too late to assume the pursuit—and he would have forfeited Muleshoe without having had a try at saving it.

They crossed the San Pedro near the fork and continued on, now bearing slightly northwest. An hour later, still in that strange silence which had settled over them, they came to the nearly dry Carretas and saw the jutting point of Spur Mountain looming up on their left.

"Not far to the Pass," Poe said then, turning his attention to the Yaqui.

Peralta nodded. More sparing than usual with words, and bordering on glumness, he said, "One hour. Day will come first. It is not good. Better we are off the desert before light."

"You figure they're watching their back trail, that it?" Harper said, striving to keep the conversation going.

"The wolf always watches his tracks. He guards against those who follow."

"Depends on which way they went after they reached the Pass. We don't know for certain they headed west for Tucson. Could've just said that to throw us—or anybody else—off."

"The tracks will not lie," The Yaqui murmured, and spurred on ahead, bringing an end to words.

Harper shrugged, vaguely irritated. He eased about on the saddle, resting his thigh and back muscles with a change of position. It would be a break if Chris and the others had lied about their destination, had instead continued on up the Animas Valley. Such would take them by the McGarrity place—and Edwina. Chris could even have had enough brass to stop and spend the night there. He was acquainted with the McGarritys, of course, and they would have no idea of what had happened in Mexico.

He grinned, hopeful that the outlaws had taken that route. He and Rojo could then swing by McGarrity's and mooch a hot meal, and he would get to see and talk to Edwina for a few minutes. He ought to explain to her what he was up against, anyway; she had a right to know, just in case he failed and lost everything.

But that wasn't going to be the way of it—not if he had to chase Chris and his bastardly friends all the way to California! There was too much at stake even to consider failure.

Daylight caught them on the broad, sloping plain that funneled up to San Luis Pass, and again Poe Harper marveled at the excellent time they were making. He watched the ground now, taking his cue from Peralta, who had begun to search for the hoofprints of the six horsemen. The wind played out shortly after that, and the bright slashes of purple-flowered loco weed and clusters of white fleabane began to show in the increasing light. There had been a shower not too many days before, and the desert was exhibiting its beauty.

The Yaqui did not locate signs of the outlaws' passage until they reached the narrow trail that led into the Pass. He lifted a brown hand and called a halt when his probing eyes eventually picked up the welter of tracks. Dismounting, he squatted on his heels and examined the indentations carefully.

"It is the ones," he announced finally. "Six horses. One of large hoof. All tired." He stared off toward the Peloncillos. "They go west—for Skeleton Canyon."

Poe sighed. He had permitted his hopes and

expectations of seeing Edwina to build too high; it was too much to expect of luck. He could forget it. The round trip to McGarrity's would mean a long forty miles out of the way, and two weeks allowance or not, he couldn't afford that kind of time. The sooner he caught up with the outlaws and herded them back to Salcedo, the better for all.

"Then I reckon it's Tucson," he said.

Peralta nodded and came upright. He did not look around—he seemed intent on something far back in the rough, brushy hills. Poe followed his gaze but saw only the gradually lightening sky.

"What is it?"

The Yaqui turned, thrust a foot into a stirrup, and swung to the saddle. "The big birds come—the scavengers. It is best we hurry."

"Buzzards?" Poe pressed, again staring into the west. "Where?"

He knew it was a useless question the instant it was voiced. Rojo had the eyes of an eagle. He could see for amazing distances. His vision was equaled only by his ability to follow a trail, to skulk silently about through the brush easily as a shadow—all a priceless heritage from his Yaqui mother. Such had been one of the reasons Harper had brought him along rather than use one of the *vaqueros,* who would be equally adept when it came to riding and shooting. That—and the fact that he considered Rojo his closest friend.

"Over the canyon," Peralta said. "I saw first but two, maybe three birds. Now there are many."

A mixture of fear and anger rose within Poe. "Apaches!" he said harshly. "The Goddamn Apaches have jumped them sure as hell!"

"It is likely so," Peralta replied in a quiet, sober way.

34

"Word came that Juh and many braves had left the father tribe to form another. They choose trails of their own. The canyon is said to be a favored place."

Juh—Chiricahua war chief, always a troublemaker. Harper stirred in angry despair. "If he's got Chris and the others, this thing could blow sky high—right in my face!" he said in a wild voice. "Let's get up there. Might not be too late . . ."

"Already it is too late," the Yaqui said. "See how the birds swing low—"

"Move out, Goddammit!" Harper shouted. "There might be a chance!"

Peralta made no answer but simply wheeled his black, touched him with spurs, and sent him loping up the trail.

Harper, plagued now with a gnawing worry, followed. He didn't know what Salcedo's reaction would be if he returned with only word that the outlaws were dead, victims of Apaches, and the gold had been lost to the braves. Perhaps he would believe—and possibly he would not, and then the net result would be the loss of Muleshoe through no fault of his own.

He'd take proof, he decided. He'd load the bodies on horses and haul them back to the Federale captain, stink and all. It would be a hell of a thing to do, but if that's what it took to save his holdings, it's what would be done. But the gold would be gone—twenty thousand dollars' worth of bad luck. He couldn't help that.

The trail grew steeper, more brushy. Chipmunks darted in and out of the glistening rocks, and once, a fat porcupine waddled across the road, frightening the Yaqui's horse. Poe kept his eyes on the sky above the ridges, still unable to locate the circling vultures. The sun was out now, bearing down full strength. The canyon pulsed with heat.

The horses slowed, the long trip from the ranch beginning to take its toll of them as they labored through the canyon. He should have called a halt when they reached the Pass, Harper knew, and taken time to eat while the animals rested. But when the Yaqui had spotted the soaring vultures he had forgotten all else but the need to hurry on and reach the scene of whatever had taken place. He pushed the thought aside; the horses could stand it a little longer—they'd have to.

They topped out the first roll of knolls and dropped into a narrow arroyo on the opposite side. The trail veered sharply, angling due north, hemmed in on both sides by buckbrush and rocks that all but glowed with the burning heat.

Eventually, they climbed from that declivity, and for a time they followed a narrow ridge. A slow breeze found them there, carrying a hint of coolness; but it was just that, barely perceptible. And then, abruptly, they were again in a deep, rock-walled pocket with the sun lashing them with breathless fury.

Poe saw the vultures. There were a dozen or more of the huge, broad-winged birds circling slowly, cautiously, and not high. They were concentrating above a point not a quarter mile distant—on the yonder side of a straight-running hogback.

"Take it slow," Harper called softly to Peralta. "Apaches could be still hanging around—if that's what this is all about."

The Yaqui bobbed his head. He pointed to the hogback. "We stop there. Then I go look."

"We'll both look," Harper said, and pulled his rifle from its boot.

When they gained the ridge, they drew off into the dense brush. Tethering the horses, they crept through the tangle of thorny mentzelia and oak to the ledge. It burned their hands as they wormed their way across it. At its rim Rojo hissed a low warning, then raised his head to look beyond. After a moment he got to his knees. Two vultures, bolder than the others, were hunched on a fallen tree directly below. They leaped into flight instantly at the Yaqui's appearance.

"There is no need for care," Peralta said, and pointed to the body of a man lying face down in a small clearing a few yards away. "The Apaches have been here and have gone."

SIX

A GRIMNESS CLAIMED POE HARPER AS HE LOOKED down upon the lifeless, battered figure. He could not tell who it was; it might be Chris. It lay partly hidden in the shadows beneath a scrub oak, head all but hidden. Throat tight, Harper slid off the ledge and trotted to the body. He squatted and rolled the man to his back. Relief slipped through Harper. It was the outlaw called Schrader—Tom Schrader. He had been shot three times, then worked over with a knife.

Poe rose to his feet and glanced around. Schrader might not be the only victim. He searched for a short time but found no others. He looked then for Rojo Peralta. The Yaqui was cruising silently about the area, his sharp eyes digging into the shadows, the dark brush pockets, and along the trail. He paused once, allowed his gaze to rest upon something of interest to him for a brief time, then moved on. When he returned to where Poe waited, his face was wooden.

37

"They go west. A big party. The others are prisoners. There are wounded."

Harper studied the Peloncillos. "Camp must be somewhere close."

"It will not be far," Rojo agreed. "A horse was killed, butchered. The Indians took with them the hindquarters."

Poe brushed at the sweat on his face and lowered his eyes to Schrader. "How long ago do you figure this happened?"

Peralta knelt beside the outlaw. After a few moments he said, "Was yesterday. Late. Before the setting of the sun."

Harper groaned. "Means those redskinned bastards had the whole night to play with them. Could all be dead by now."

The Yaqui stirred his shoulders. "Perhaps it is better," he said softly.

"Better!" Poe flared at him. "If they're dead, it'll probably cost me Muleshoe!"

Peralta did not flinch before Harper's withering fury. "It is still so."

Poe's impatience soared. "What the hell's eating you, Rojo? You've had something sticking in your gullet ever since we started. Spit it out! Let's hear it!"

The Yaqui's eyes were steady. His ruddy skin was drawn tight over the bones of his skull. "I say only that if a man must die, it is better it not be by the hand of his kin."

"Figured that was it. You think I'm wrong to turn Chris over to the Mexican Government."

"I think only your heart has become a prisoner of the curse."

"Curse!" Poe echoed. "Don't jabber your old woman's tales at me! Nothing but a lot of talk."

38

"I have spoken my belief," the Yaqui said stiffly, and wheeled about. "I bring the horses, *patrón.*"

Patrón! So it was no longer *compañero* but *patrón,* the more distant term of respect. Poe throttled the angry words that surged to his throat. If it were anyone but Rojo Peralta, he'd send the man packing. But he needed the Yaqui, at least until they tracked down the Apaches and found out for certain about the rest of the outlaws— and the gold.

He could understand Peralta's thinking, however; he had not lived a lifetime in Mexico without becoming aware of the value they set on family ties. They were sentimentalists in that respect, and one of the kin, no matter his faults or how serious his crime, was still of the kin and must be treated as such . . .

"To hell with that," Poe muttered aloud, and looked back up the canyon. Loyalty of that sort was fine—up to a point. He brought his glance back to Tom Schrader. The body had to be buried; they couldn't just ride off and leave Schrader there for the buzzards and coyotes to feast on.

He cast about until he located a shallow wash a few yards off the trail. Taking the outlaw by the feet, he dragged him into the narrow depression and began to pile rocks and litter over him. Before he had completed the chore Peralta, tight-lipped and looking down, returned with the horses. He anchored the animals to a juniper and moved in to aid Harper. When they finished Schrader was safe from the scavengers.

The stiffness between Harper and the Yaqui was more pronounced now. It was like an invisible wall over which neither could climb.

"We keep moving," Harper said. "Ought to find that

39

Apache camp somewhere around. Can't give Chris and the others up for dead until we know for sure."

"*Si, patrón*," the Yaqui murmured, and moved to his horse.

Poe watched him wheel away, feeling now the first pangs of remorse. They had been close friends—like brothers, in fact—since the beginning. Now they were strangers. He saw the Yaqui go to the saddle, settle himself, and wait in patient silence. Anger suddenly seized control. The devil with Rojo Peralta! If he wanted to feel that way about it—let him! He wasn't the one who stood to lose a fine ranch, a lifetime of work—of hopes and dreams.

He stamped across the clearing to the bay and jerked the reins savagely from the juniper. Mounting, he snapped. "Let's go!" and whirled back onto the trail.

They pressed on, riding deeper into the mountains while the heat increased with the steadily climbing sun. Around noon they halted to rest the horses and took advantage of that pause to eat—in dead silence—a portion of the food Carmelita had prepared. They did not build a fire for coffee, fearing that the smoke or the smell of it might attract the Apaches, who could be nearby.

They eased the horses' thirst from their canteens and moved on an hour later, both grim, each wrapped in his own firm beliefs and convictions. The heat in the canyon was by then sweltering, almost unbearable, and to breathe was an effort. But they rode on, and at midafternoon they broke out of the hills onto the Arizona side. Immediately they saw the smoke from the Indian camp.

The spirals lifted upward from the near tip of the Guadalupe Mountains, a small range to the south. There were a half a dozen curls winding into the steel-blue sky, and Poe reckoned it was a fair-sized village. He beckoned to Peralta.

"We'll move in from the back side of the hills," he said, pointing at the Guadalupes. "Ought to be able to see good from there."

The Yaqui nodded and immediately swung his horse to the left and began to angle across a narrow plain toward the distant slopes. Keeping the ragged formation between them and the smoke, they approached from the east. They found no trail up the side of the mountains, and it required a long, hot hour's work to gain the crest. It was late in the afternoon when they pulled to a halt. Dismounting, they tied the weary horses to a bramble of mesquite, heavily hung with golden-yellow pods, and bellied their way to where they could look upon the village.

There were two dozen or more wickiups scattered in a loose circle around a clearing to form a sort of plaza. A few squaws and small children stirred indolently in the blazing sun. The knot of horses gathered in a brush corral proved that the men were there, however, likely keeping to their shelters during the heat.

Poe felt the Yaqui tug at his arm, heard him say, "See—behind the far wickiup . . ."

Harper followed his leveled finger. Five horses, still saddled and bridled, stood hipshot beyond the farthermost shelter. It proved what they had assumed; the Apaches had taken prisoner the rest of the party. Hope lifted within Poe. The outlaws could still be alive—and maybe the Indians hadn't discovered the gold yet, since the horses had not been stripped of their gear. Urgency began to crowd Harper.

"Wonder where they've got Chris and the rest," he

said, his eyes moving from shelter to shelter. "Got to be in one of the wickiups."

Peralta said, "Where the horses stand, there they will be. It is a way of torture. Escape is near—only a step away—yet it is not possible. But for one there will be no escape. Look."

Again Harper followed the Yaqui's forefinger. At the north edge of the camp, between two of the crude brush huts, a man lay spread-eagled on the sand. He was dead, his sightless eyes staring into the pitiless sun. Poe winced, fear once more clawing at him. At this distance he could not tell which of the outlaws it was. Likely it was one of those wounded back in the canyon. The Apaches would want to have their sport before he died.

"Is it Chris?" he asked.

"No, *patrón,*" Peralta replied. "It is the one with the light hair."

Harper relaxed slightly. That would be Bradley. Four left now. Chris, Wyatt, Vickery, and the skinny one named Barney Johnson—assuming none of those was already dead and left somewhere along the trail for the vultures.

He glanced anxiously at the sun. Still a full hour until setting, then a second hour after that before it became dark enough to move about safely. If Rojo were right and the remaining outlaws were being held prisoner in the wickiup where the horses stood, there would be no chance of getting to them until full dark, when the camp quieted down.

They were in for a hot, tedious wait—and perhaps a bloody one if the Apaches ran true to form. They would spend the evening making sport of one or more of their captives.

Poe's jaw hardened. Chris could be one of those

chosen to provide the entertainment. He felt a growing uneasiness; could he lie there and watch his own brother being tortured to death? It seemed different, somehow, compared with handing him over to Salcedo.

He turned to one side, wiped sweat from his face, and studied Peralta. "Any chance of slipping down there to that wickiup and getting them out? Braves all seem to be asleep. Squaws don't appear to be paying much attention to anything."

The Yaqui shook his head. "No. Such is not possible. There is much open ground." He paused, frowning. "The men come now. It is time for eating."

Poe turned his attention back to the camp. Three braves had appeared and were sauntering toward the fires where the women were preparing the evening meal in several blackened pots. While he watched, other Apaches came into sight, emerging from the dark interiors of wickiups, yawning and stretching.

The men began to feed themselves, reaching into the steaming kettles for chunks of meat, handling the scalding bits gingerly, tossing them back and forth as they allowed the meat to cool. Now and then one paused to kick at the dozen or more dogs hovering about.

Poe counted thirty men in all, equally as many women and children. Juh had not recruited a very large following, but the ones who had heeded his call were all fierce-looking men—probably the worst of the renegades. Undoubtedly the army and many ranchers, as well as other tribes, were in for considerable trouble.

Harper glanced about. The ragged shelf upon which they sprawled was uncomfortable from the day's stored heat and from sharp-edged rocks embedded in its surface. There was no shade nearby, other than low creosote bushes, snakeweed clumps, and even lower growth. Poe scanned the area behind and to the sides; it was the same. There was no point in moving.

"Soon as it's dark we'll get down to that wickiup," he said, settling back.

"The night will come too late," the Yaqui murmured. "Already they begin."

Harper hurriedly swung his eyes to the camp. Two Apaches were dragging a man toward the center of the plaza.

SEVEN

A YELL ECHOED THROUGH THE STIFLING CALM. THE braves clustered around the pots rose, licked their greasy fingers, wiped them on the filthy, once-white drawers they wore, and fell in with the procession. Women and children, several pausing hastily to seize a morsel of food from the kettles, also joined the parade.

"*Pobrecito*," Peralta breathed softly, and crossed himself.

Poor devil is right, Harper thought. What lay ahead for him—and the other captives—would not be pretty. It would be better if the outlaw, whoever he was, could die now.

Poe considered his rifle and the possibility of ending the man's misery and pain with a well-placed bullet. It would be a foolhardy move. To reveal their presence on the ridge would bring the Apaches surging up for them instantly—and everything would be lost. He could do but one thing—sit tight and when the time came, rescue as many of the outlaws as possible—along with the gold. Half the wanted party should satisfy Salcedo.

The Indians halted in the center of the plaza. The two

44

braves dragging the prisoner released their grip. The unconscious man sprawled, onto the sunbaked ground. It was not Chris. The outlaw was too tall and thin. Poe thought it might be the one named Johnson, but in the gradually fading light and because of the distance, he could not be certain.

From the side of the camp nearest the mountains, two more Apaches appeared. They carried between them a small tree. All but two of the branches had been hacked from its trunk, leaving it roughly in the shape of a cross. As they approached, other braves began to dig a hole, apparently for the sapling. Johnson was to be tied to the stake. At that Harper frowned; Apaches generally didn't go in for torture by burning. It was too quick. They preferred dragging death out to a final, exhausted gasp.

"What the hell they up to?" he muttered, half-aloud.

"*Tiro al blanco,*" the Yaqui replied. "For the young ones."

Target practice—literally. Poe felt his flesh crawl. Where his *vaqueros* and American cowboys used old bottles and such to sharpen their marksmanship, the Apaches chose live targets—an enemy when available. Johnson would be tied to the tree and the boys of the tribe would be permitted to shoot arrows into his body, taking instructions from the older, more experienced braves during the process. It was nothing other than a lesson in the art of killing.

Poe Harper again considered his rifle. A tough man, hardened to death as much as any, he was not sure he could stand by and watch another methodically slaughtered.

More shouts drifted across the clearing. There was sudden confusion at one of the fires. Someone had

45

stumbled into the leg of a pole tripod from which a kettle was suspended and overturned it. Dogs were swarming in for the treat. Two of the squaws seized lengths of firewood and began to flail about wildly, endeavoring to drive the starved brutes away. The camp paused to watch, braves laughing uproariously at the women's frantic efforts, while other squaws looked on sympathetically.

The dogs at last scattered, and, with the meat rescued and again in the righted kettle, the Apaches resumed the task of erecting the tree. They placed the sapling in the hole, stamped the dry earth into place about it, and made it firm. That done, the prisoner was hauled to his feet and lashed into an upright position, ropes holding him to the trunk and cross limbs.

It was Johnson, Poe saw, frankly relieved. Not because of the outlaw's misfortune at being first chosen, but because it was not Chris. Johnson was conscious now. He raised his head and stared about at the ring of painted, grinning faces. His mouth worked angrily, but what words he spoke were lost in the distance.

In a group the Apaches moved back to the opposite end of the clearing. More wood was tossed into the fires, and the shadowing area brightened. A dozen or so boys drew together, ranging in age from those scarcely able to walk, to thin, wiry young braves of fifteen or sixteen. Each possessed a bow and a handful of arrows. They congregated before a wickiup from which the remnants of an old cavalry guidon hung limply above the entrance.

Older men drifted in and formed a half-circle around the boys, some squatting, some standing with arms folded across their copper-colored chests. A few women paused to watch, but most went on about their drudgery, paying no mind to the activities.

The coyote skin draped over the entrance to the wickiup before which the crowd had assembled was drawn back. A short, lean Apache, band around his forehead, coarse hair hanging below his shoulders, stepped into the open. He paused for a time and looked around, arrogance setting him apart from the others who turned to face him.

"It is Juh," Peralta said.

Harper watched the war chief stalk into the midst of the boys. He swept them with his glance, then touched the smallest of the lot on the head.

"He is youngest. He is honored with the first shot," the Yaqui explained. "Now he makes the choice of others."

Juh went through the group, placing his hand on each of the boys, following a system that permitted the youngest to have first chance at the white prisoner-target, working up to the eldest, whose turn would come last. When the ritual was completed, he stepped back to the doorway of his shelter and took up a haughty stance in front of it.

More fuel was thrown to the flames, and the plaza brightened. The smallest of the boys was pushed forward amid a vast amount of laughter. The youngster fitted an arrow to his bow, drew back the string, and released the shaft. It fell a dozen paces short. More shouts and laughter broke out as the boy was hustled to one side while the next contestant was shoved to the fore.

Propelled by a somewhat larger bow, the second marksman's arrow traveled the necessary distance but went wide of the struggling, cursing Johnson. The boy was quickly brushed aside while the third, a much older Apache youth, claimed his turn.

Poe knew there would be no lucky miss for Barney Johnson this time. The manner in which the Apache handled his weapon bespoke training and some experience. He took deliberate aim and loosed his arrow. It struck the outlaw in the belly, drove deep into his body. A yell burst across the clearing as the shaft quivered in the dancing firelight. Johnson stiffened, sagged.

There was much backslapping as the youth jauntily moved away from the mark, making room for the next participant, who raised his bow and started to aim. Conversation rose. The boy hesitated. Evidently some wagering was to be done.

It was soon settled, and the young brave again prepared to shoot. He was using a metal-tipped arrow. Poe saw the glitter of light upon the point. He started to make a comment on it to Peralta, but at that instant the slim shaft was released. It sped into Johnson's breast, wrenching a shrill cry of pain from his contorted lips. He struggled futilely to free himself from the tree; finally he gave it up and hung there limply. Shouting and laughter were echoing through the camp as bets were settled and a fifth Apache took his position.

He was all business, wasting no time. He raised his bow, fired quickly, and stepped back. His arrow also found its mark in the outlaw's chest, very near the other. Johnson barely moved at the impact, and Harper wondered if the man was dead. It would be merciful. Several more boys had yet to try their skill. Each could be expected to be more proficient than his predecessor.

Poe turned his face from the brutal scene, sickened by

what he saw. It was death in its most savage form, but to the Apaches' way of thinking, it was merely just treatment for a hated enemy. There was no such word as cruelty in the Apache mind; a man was fearless, an expert thief, and a merciless captor. Such marked him as a true brave and worthy warrior entitled to the respect and admiration of all Apaches. Kindness to others—and self—was no favoring quality; rather, it was a weakness not to be tolerated. A man's stature was gauged by the number of enemies he had slain, horses he had stolen, wives he had taken, and offspring he had sired. Nothing else counted in the tribal scheme.

It was a way of life, and Poe Harper, realizing this, had some glimmer of understanding of Apache values. But it made it a no less horrifying sight, and he was glad when he again gazed down into the clearing and upon the pathetic, slumped figure that had been Barney Johnson, looking now much like an elongated pincushion, and saw that he was dead.

The group in front of Juh's wickiup had dissolved, and fires were being allowed to burn out. Several of the smaller boys, standing at close range, continued to drive arrows into the lifeless body of the outlaw, but the majority of the Apaches were drifting off to bed. Poe sighed with relief. The evening's festivities were over. The remaining captives were to be saved for later.

Harper turned his attention to the shelter where the prisoners were being held. A brave, rifle in hand, was settling down before the draped entrance, sitting cross-legged, weapon athwart his knees. Another was dragging up surplus wood to the centermost fire. He would be the sentry. Two men on guard duty . . . Juh apparently feared no trouble.

Poe glanced about. The night was filled with the pale

glow of stars. It would not be too difficult to enter the camp. Later, when the moon came out, it would not be so easy. He pulled himself to his knees, careful not to become silhouetted against the skyline. He was stiff and cramped from the hours of lying nearly motionless on the rough surface of the ledge.

"Let's get down there," he said. "Be a lot brighter later on."

Peralta, who had also drawn away from the lip of the bench, now studied the camp. "It is so. It is also better we stay on this side of the hills until we are below the wickiups. From there we can cross. The breeze comes from the north. The dogs will not smell and become alarmed."

Harper nodded. He had not considered that danger. The Yaqui missed nothing. He was fortunate to have him along, and he wished suddenly that the misunderstanding that had risen between them could be wiped away and the high, invisible wall that lay between them could be torn down. Rojo Peralta was his friend—actually his best friend. It was not good to have things the way they were.

"You are right as always, *compañero*," he said softly. "Lead out."

But the Yaqui's tone was stiff and impersonal as ever when he answered, "*Sí, patrón.*"

EIGHT

THE YAQUI FOLLOWED A COURSE THAT LED THEM down the slope of the mountain to the sandy plain below before he swung southward. In this manner he avoided the loose rock and the resultant far-reaching sound of metal horseshoes striking against stone. In the stillness of the night such could easily be heard in the Apache camp despite its distant location.

Out of the hills, Peralta pegged the pace at a steady lope, and a half hour later, in a deep gash in the side of the Guadalupes, he again veered right and began to thread his way to the crest of the mountain. Quiet passage once more was a necessity, as they were bearing toward Juh's village, and progress was slow and careful.

When they finally crossed the low-lying chain of bluffs and peaks and broke out onto the mesa to the west, the tip of the moon was just pushing above the horizon behind them.

Their task would be more difficult now. Poe had hoped they might make their way to the wickiup while it was yet comparatively dark; under the bright, flooding light, and with the camp placed well out on the flat, their chances of being seen were more than doubled.

He said nothing to Peralta. The Yaqui would have realized that too, and he was likely already searching his mind for a way to offset the disadvantage.

They came in sight of the camp a few minutes later, the shelters throwing dark, square outlines against the pale, fluttering glow of the sentry's fire. Immediately Rojo halted and slipped from the saddle.

"It is better we walk."

Poe dropped to the ground. The dull clink of his spurs reminded him that they were still on his heels, and he took time to remove them and place them in his saddlebags to ensure silence. Touching the butt of his pistol to be certain it was in place, and feeling the long-bladed knife in his belt, he stepped out ahead of his

51

horse, leading the bay by short rein. The Yaqui was a few paces in front of him.

They approached the camp from the southwest, walking slowly and with care. The dogs would be their greatest threat; once aware of intruders the pack of mongrels would set up such a racket that the entire camp would be aroused. But with the light breeze against their faces, Poe knew the odds for going undetected were good unless ill luck brought them accidentally into contact with one of the lean brutes.

A hundred yards from the first shelter Rojo paused and pointed to the left. Glancing in that direction Harper saw a shallow arroyo in which the irregularly shaped formation of brush laid a dark splash on the land. He understood at once the Yaqui's thinking; it would be a good place to leave the horses. They would not be completely hidden, but standing in the mesquite, or whatever the tangle of growth was, they would blend and not be noticeable.

They swung aside to the sandy wash, tethered the horses, and now, crouched, made their way directly toward the camp. The odor of greasewood smoke was in the air, mingling with the strong, rank smell of the village itself. Somewhere on the slopes of the Guadalupes an owl hooted, the call lonely and forlorn in the hush. The moon broke into full blush at that moment, spreading its silver mist over the flat, and Poe Harper had the sudden, uncomfortable feeling of being fully exposed. Instinctively, he hunkered lower.

He peered ahead. The horses that had been standing at the rear of the prison wickiup had been removed, apparently taken to where the tribe's *remuda* was being held. He wondered if they were moving in the right direction, toward the correct shelter—then recalled that

52

it had been the one next the end. He glanced at Peralta; the Yaqui was slanting for that particular one.

They drew in behind the wickiup. Somewhere in the camp, on its far side, dogs were fighting over the leavings of the evening meal, their snarls and yelps the only sounds to break the stillness. Poe drew his knife. To use a gun, should they be noted by the sentry or the guard, would be fatal. The silent effectiveness of a sharp blade was in order here.

Peralta worked in closer to the wickiup. He placed his ear to the rough, brushy wall. Moonlight struck across his high-boned face, lighting the angles, deepening the pockets, and for a few moments he appeared to be a carved image of some sort while he listened. Then he shook his head and, on hands and knees, began to make his way around the circular shelter. Poe eased quietly in beside him. Shoulder to shoulder they crept to where they could see the entrance.

The guard sat as they had last seen him, cross-legged, rifle resting on his knees. He was sleeping, head forward, chin resting on his chest. The brave at the fire also dozed in the wavering flare of the flames. The dogs still wrangled over the bones.

Rojo touched Harper's arm and made a slight motion with his hand directing the young rancher to remain where he was. Not waiting to see if Poe understood, the Yaqui pulled away. Flat on his belly, he squirmed in close to the side of the wickiup and edged toward the sleeping guard. He reached the Apache. Poe saw him rise slightly, saw the glint of moonlight on steel as the Yaqui struck. The guard toppled soundlessly.

Peralta stared at the brave's crumpled shape for several moments, then moved into the wickiup. He emerged after a brief time and crawled back to Poe.

"It is empty," he whispered. "All have gone." He twisted about, pointed to the Apache. "Already he was dead. A knife had been thrust into his back."

Harper choked back a grunt of surprise. Chris and the other two men had somehow escaped. It would have been sometime after the camp had quieted down—after their horses had been led away and the guard had taken his position in front of the shelter. Chris or one of the other men had managed to conceal a knife, had used it on the Apache to gain freedom.

Poe swore softly, feeling a mixture of relief for their escape and dismay at their slipping through his fingers. He glanced at Peralta. The Yaqui was looking toward the center of the camp. The sentry had roused and was now upright adding wood to his dwindling fire.

"We go," the Yaqui murmured. "Quick, *patrón*."

Immediately he began to back his way between the two wickiups, never removing his eyes from the sentry, who had turned and was staring in their direction. He was not looking at them, Poe realized, but at the recumbent figure of the guard. Harper moved after Peralta, not taking time to turn about but simply pulling himself deeper into the shadows that lay between the shelters, as did the Yaqui.

He heard the Apache call out. It was in Spanish but a word he did not understand. The brave was becoming curious. He yelled a second time, his voice guarded and low—and much nearer. Harper and Peralta, finally behind the shelters, leaped to their feet. Wheeling, they raced across the open ground for the horses.

The alarm caught them before they had covered half the distance.

A loud yell brought answering shouts from the wickiups. Dogs began to bark, and by the time they had

54

gained the arroyo, the Apache camp was in an uproar. Fires began to blaze up. The clearing echoed with voices.

Poe and the Yaqui vaulted to their saddles and spun about. There was no need, no time, to lead the horses. Their one hope was to get as far from the camp as possible, and quickly.

"Head for the mountain!" Poe shouted as they streaked across the flat.

NINE

THEY RACED FOR THE SHADOWY, BULKING GUADALUPES. Confusion had increased in the Apache camp, and the night was filled with the shouts of Indians and the frantic barking of dogs. Poe Harper flung a glance toward the irregular line of wickiups. Figures ran back and forth between them, outlined against the firelight.

He turned his eyes forward. The first outcropping of brush and rock was only yards away. Peralta's voice reached him.

"Horses! They come quick now!"

Harper looked again to the encampment. Riders were streaming from an opening between two of the shelters, dark shapes bent low over their ponies. They were lining out due south, evidently believing that their escaping prisoners had taken that direction. It dawned on Poe Harper in that moment that the Apaches did not actually know of their presence; they assumed he and Rojo were the men they had imprisoned in the wickiup. He couldn't make up his mind whether the error was to their advantage or not—and there was no time to ponder it.

55

Harper reached the brush-covered knolls at the base of the mountains a length ahead of the Yaqui. Immediately he cut the heaving bay to the left and plunged recklessly into a stand of screening ironwood and jojoba. He allowed the horse to rush on for another hundred yards or so, then drew him to a halt. Peralta rushed in beside him. Both horses were laboring for breath. In their worn condition it had been a grueling dash.

Poe raised himself in his stirrups and stared toward the mesa. A quarter mile distant he could see blurred motion in the muted silver night. The Apaches had turned and were doubling back. He wheeled to Peralta and started to speak, but the Yaqui lifted his hand in an abrupt command for silence. Poe cocked his ear into the quiet.

To the east he heard the faint drumming of fast-running horses. He frowned and thought, *More Apaches*. But he doubted that.

"Chris. And his *amigos*," the Yaqui guessed. "They go back."

It was Poe's first opportunity to think of his brother. After they discovered the escape, matters had developed so rapidly that there had been no time for anything but frenzied flight.

Apparently Chris, if he still lived, and the others—possibly three men, perhaps fewer, since there was no way of knowing how many were dead—had been able to recover their horses and get well away from the Apache camp before the alarm was sounded.

But assuming Peralta was correct and the receding hoofbeats were those of the outlaw party, why would they double back to Skeleton Canyon? It didn't make sense. It had been their intention to reach Tucson—in

56

the exact opposite direction. Why the change in plan?

There could be only one answer to that, Poe concluded. The outlaws figured their best chance for escape lay in running for the nearby hills, rather than the Swisshelm Mountains, a good fifteen miles on to the west. If true, it was a lucky break for him; the outlaws—and, he hoped, the gold—would be that much closer to the border and the waiting Luis Salcedo when he again caught up with them.

"Let's get after—" he began, impatient to be on their trail—and then hushed instantly as Rojo hissed a soft warning.

He looked around. Three braves, walking their horses, were moving by. They were silent, intent shadows in the halflight, less than a hundred feet away.

Harper felt the hair rise on the back of his neck. The Indians had made absolutely no sound in their approach. The effectiveness of unshod hooves in loose sand was unquestioned in his mind now. Motionless, hoping neither his bay nor Peralta's black would make any abrupt move, Poe watched the Apaches drift by, dully shining ghosts in the night.

When they were well beyond the brush, he again lifted himself in his stirrups and made a long, slow study of the slope above them. If there were Indians that close—there would be others. A few moments later he knew he was not wrong. Farther up on the hillside a horse grunted as it made a misstep. It added up to one thing; the Apaches had cut back and were now combing the hills.

Locked by tension, Poe rode out the taut moments. He wiped at the sweat gathered on his brow and grinned tightly into the dark shadows of the night. They were trapped—caught in the center of a bunch of prowling,

57

blood-lusting savages. The bastards were everywhere. There was no way to go—no direction in which they could find safety.

"*Patrón* . . ." The Yaqui's hoarse whisper, was barely audible. "This way—follow."

Peralta brought his horse about quietly, angling toward the edge of the brush. Poe stared at the hunched shape of the breed for a few seconds in amazement, and then he understood the wisdom of the move. They would fall in behind the searching Apaches, strung out in a wide line across the slope and flat. Literally, they would join them, become two of the hunters instead of the hunted.

"The hat," Peralta murmured.

Instantly Harper pulled off his wide-brimmed headpiece and crammed it under his leg. Their gear, of course, would also be a giveaway should anyone take particular note; but if an Apache drew near enough to discern that discrepancy, it would be time to fight.

They moved on, seeing more Indians higher up on the slope and others flung out onto the desert. They came abreast of the camp. Poe's muscles tightened, and his nerves began to sing as they moved into the flickering, outreaching flare of the fires. It required endless time, it seemed, to ride through the glow, but finally they were beyond it and again in the semidarkness of moon and starlight. No outcry had been raised. They had passed unnoticed.

A mile later a shout echoed through the night. Instantly Rojo veered toward the mountains and their protective rocks and pockets of brush.

"They come this way now," he said over his shoulder. "The hunt is finished. They wait for the sun. It is best we hide until they have passed."

If they pass, Poe thought, following the Yaqui into the tangled undergrowth. They halted well back from open ground. Higher up on the mountain, displaced gravel spilled slowly off a ledge. To their left the muted plodding of other horses across the sand reached them. They were once more surrounded as the braves made their way back to the camp. Tense, soaked with sweat, Poe Harper waited.

There was a dull thud immediately ahead, beyond Peralta. Harper stiffened. One of the Apaches was close, apparently moving directly toward them.

He saw the Yaqui reach for his knife, saw its long blade glitter as he brought it into the open. The sound came again. Another—this one a short distance *up* the slope. A second Apache!

Harper's scalp tingled. He drew his pistol. A knife would be of little use if they were confronted suddenly by several braves.

The long head of a horse bobbed into view, coming from behind a large boulder. An instant later an Apache, face tipped down in weariness, appeared. The horse came on, then halted sharply when it drew abreast of Peralta's black. The brave roused, glancing up. At that instant the Yaqui lunged forward and struck, driving his knife deep into the Apache's throat.

There was a choked gasp, a gurgle as the Apache died. His horse shied off into the brush. Then followed a dull thump as the dead warrior fell to the ground. Instantly a guttural voice called from the slope.

"Que pasa?"

Sinking back onto his saddle, Peralta answered,

"Es nada . . . Vamonos."

Harper sat in rigid silence, not sure the Apache was satisfied with the reply. Moments later he heard the

59

clatter of loose shale a short distance below and breathed easier. The brave had believed and continued on his way. Again he brushed at the sweat on his face and glanced to Rojo Peralta. The Yaqui's features were impassive. He nodded, touched his horse with his heels, and moved out. Poe followed.

They rode at a deliberate walk for a full mile and then urged their tired horses into a lope, heading them back toward the Peloncillos and Skeleton Canyon. Still wondering, and doubting slightly that it had been the outlaws they had heard earlier, Harper caught up with Peralta.

"Not sure this is right. Could have been somebody else riding this way. Maybe Indians. Just doesn't figure Chris and his pals would turn back."

The Yaqui shrugged. "Soon we reach the place where the trail narrows. I look for tracks of the horses. Then we know."

Satisfied, Poe fell silent. It was the only way they could be sure. By coincidence, of course, there could be other riders moving east, but the Yaqui would be able to tell if it were a different party. His first study of the outlaws' horses' hoofprints that morning in the Pass had established their characteristics in his mind. He could tell instantly if they were following the wrong party.

They saw no more Apaches as they moved steadily on through the silver-shot night. The long hours were beginning to tell on Poe Harper now, and he was feeling hunger. They should halt soon, to eat and to rest the horses as well as themselves. But the possibility of the outlaws' being only an hour or so ahead pushed that need to the back of his mind. There would be plenty of time to sleep, to take it easy once they had caught up with Chris and the others and he had his hands on them and the Sabine gold.

It was still dark when they reached the trail that led directly into the mountains. Harper halted beside Peralta, who swung down from the black and began to examine the soft earth. He had only the light of the moon and stars to go by, but after three or four minutes, he straightened up, his face set to satisfied lines.

"Three riders, *patrón.* They pass this way."

"You sure it's Chris—the men we want?"

The Yaqui moved his slight shoulders. "Of this I am certain. One horse has the big hoof. The same as before when we see them in the Pass."

Harper looked up, toward the crest. His expression was harsh. "Can't be far ahead. Let's get after them."

Peralta did not move. He shook his head. "It is better we first rest the horses. They are tired . . ."

"Hell with that!" Poe snapped, goaded by a relentless impatience. "I'm not letting that bunch slip through my hands again!"

He kicked his heels into the flanks of the bay, wishing he had taken time to dig out his spurs, and moved on. The Yaqui watched him for a brief time; then, sighing, he mounted and followed.

They reached the ragged confines of Skeleton Canyon shortly after daylight. There were no signs of the outlaws. Harper grudgingly delayed a half hour to breathe the horses and strap on his spurs, and then they pushed on.

The descent was easier on the worn animals, and they reached the fork in the road in fair time. Poe, halting on a narrow bluff, began an immediate check of the farflung country. To the south lay Mexico; Chris and his

61

friends would not head that way, so he ignored it. To the east—

"There is dust," Peralta broke into his thoughts quietly. He had pulled up a little to the left on the butte. "It is the road to Lordsburg."

Poe hurriedly shifted his gaze to the northwest, to the trail that followed along the foot of the Animas Mountains and ended some sixty miles farther on, at the settlement.

"It is them," Rojo said, studying the not too distant roll of gray dust. "Three men."

Harper cursed bitterly. He was so near—no more than an hour behind the outlaws—but considering the condition of his horse, and that of the Yaqui, it might as well be the length of a day.

He wheeled the bay off the bluff, angry and irritable, and rode him down into a shaded clearing in a pocket of brush. Dismounting, he began to jerk at the saddle cinch. He loosened it to allow the horse more comfort. Peralta pulled up nearby and fell to work on his gear.

"One hour," Harper said, his tone hard. "That's all the time we're wasting here. We'll cook up a bite to eat, rest the horses—then we're moving on. I'll be Goddamned if Chris and those bastards are getting past Lordsburg!"

TEN

IT WAS WELL NIGH MIDNIGHT WHEN POE HARPER AND the Yaqui rode into Lordsburg's narrow, curving main street. The night was cool, and the glow from the heavens softened the square edges of the buildings, rounded the ugly rock formations, and gave the settlement a stark, lonely beauty.

The business houses had closed, but the half a dozen saloons were open, yellow light from their lamps spilling through dust-streaked windows and open doorways to lay squares and oblongs upon the road. Poe turned his weary bay toward the first in line of those structures. In one he could expect to find Chris and his companions.

At the first and the second he drew blanks; but coming to the third, a small, weathered building upon the facade of which hung the sign: THE CROWSFOOT, he found the three men.

Halting in the entrance, Harper let his glance touch the outlaws. Chris, Dan Wyatt, and the gunfighter, Hart Vickery. They had been the lucky ones, he thought. Dropping his hand to the .45 at his hip, he started for the corner where the trio hunched over a table, a bottle between them. He felt Peralta at his side, paused, glanced at the Yaqui while anger simmered sullenly through him.

"Yeah?"

"This is something you must do?" the Yaqui asked. "This thing—it is right?"

"It's right," Poe said curtly, and moved deeper into the shadowy room.

The bartender looked up questioningly. Harper shook his head. Two patrons at the bar half-turned, gave him a long stare, then resumed their positions. There were no others about. Poe moved on and halted at the table. Chris screwed about in his chair and glanced to Poe. His eyes widened.

"For Christ's sake—what're you doing here?"

"You know damned well why I'm here!" Harper

shouted, instantly furious. "Twenty thousand dollars' worth of gold—and four murders!"

Wyatt came up sharply. His eyes travelled hurriedly about the room in nervous flight. "No point telling the whole country," he said.

A forced smile parted Harper's lips—one of relief. "Then the Apaches didn't get it."

Chris stared. "You over there too?"

"We were," Poe snapped. "Been following you ever since you left Muleshoe."

A stillness came over Wyatt. He was a dark-faced man, and in the poor light his features were almost indiscernible.

"You're trailing us. Why?"

Poe allowed his hand to rest on the butt of his pistol. Rojo Peralta moved a step to one side in a slow, catlike way.

"I'm taking you and that gold back to Mexico. The Federales are waiting at the ranch . . . "

Wyatt's eyes closed slowly, opened lazily. Hart Vickery stared, his flat expression revealing nothing. Only Chris displayed reaction. He leaned forward on his chair, glancing first at the Yaqui, then at Poe.

"What the hell's this all about? What's the Federales got to do with you?"

"They're holding me responsible for you—and your Goddamned friends there. And that gold!" Poe replied angrily, his voice rising. "If I don't bring you back—I lose Muleshoe. Now do you understand?"

There was a long minute of dead silence. Dan Wyatt's sardonic tone broke the hush. "So you're trading us for a lousy ranch, that it?"

"That's exactly what I'm doing," Poe flared. "I'm not losing what I spent a lifetime building up for you or anybody else!"

64

Wyatt shifted his gaze to Chris. "Fine brother you got there, kid. The Mex's will hang us higher'n a kite if they get their hands on us. Reckon you know that."

Chris frowned and looked down at the dusty floor. "Sure didn't figure to get you in trouble, Poe. I'm sorry about—"

"Being sorry's not enough!" Harper cut in coldly. "It never has been, and I'm sick of hearing you say it. Now, where's that gold? I want it put in a safe place until morning; then we're heading back to the border."

"You turning us over to the town marshal?" Vickery asked, breaking his silence.

Poe considered the question. He shrugged. "Only if you force me to. Don't want any complications with the law here. Better if Rojo and I handle it."

Vickery nodded. "Appreciate that," he said, his tone faintly mocking. He slanted a hooded look at Wyatt. "Reckon he's got us cold, Dan."

Wyatt settled back. He reached for the bottle and poured himself a drink. In the tense hush that lay across the room the gurgling of the liquor seemed enormously loud. Twirling the glass between his fingers, he studied it.

"Shame," he murmured. "Sure hate losing out on that gold, after all the trouble we went to." He glanced to Harper. "Any chance you changing your mind? We'd cut you and your Mex friend there in for a share. We got us only a three-way split now, instead of six."

The sarcasm edging Wyatt's voice sent new anger racing through Poe Harper. "Don't give me that!" he snarled. "I'll take no horsing around from you. I want the whole twenty thousand—and you along with it."

Wyatt turned to Chris. "What about it, kid? He's your brother."

Chris shook his head. "Sure hate causing him some

trouble—like losing his ranch." He hesitated, then added, "How do you and Hart feel about it?"

"We'll leave it up to you," Vickery drawled, and pushing back his chair, he got to his feet. "Ain't so sure I want to go back to Mexico, howsomever."

"Maybe, if the gold's returned . . ."

"Maybe," Wyatt said.

Poe watched them with burning eyes. They were stringing him along, making sport of his demands. They had no intention of complying with his request—none of them. He reached forward suddenly and snatched Vickery's pistol from its holster.

"All right!" he snapped, moving back a step. "I've had enough of this. I want that gold, and I want it now. And just so's things will work better, we'll head for the border tonight. Be easier to keep an eye on you."

Hart Vickery leaned back against the wall, his face quiet and set. Wyatt rose slowly. The two men at the bar wheeled about, hurriedly crossed the room, and disappeared into the street.

The bartender was a rigid shape behind his counter. "Don't want no trouble in here, mister," he said in an anxious voice.

"There'll be none," Poe replied. "Just keep out of the way." He ducked his head at Peralta. "Get Wyatt's gun. And Chris's."

Dan Wyatt half-turned. His movements were slow, lazy. He smiled at the Yaqui. "Why, sure, Mex. Here's my iron—"

With a sudden motion he completed the turn. His arm swept down, then up. His shoulder came in hard against the Yaqui, bowling him over. In that same fragment of time, he fired. The saloon rocked with the explosion. Poe, holding Vickery's pistol, replied

66

instantly. Wyatt jolted, staggered back against the wall, buckled forward.

Hart Vickery yelled. He seized the edge of the table, shoved it into Poe Harper, and lunged. Poe went down as the table smashed into him. He fell against Peralta, drove him back to the floor. Harper jerked his head to one side as Vickery aimed a fist at his jaw. He took the blow on his neck, grunting from the pain. He felt the pistol wrenched from his fingers, heard Vickery yell again.

"Come on, kid! He ain't hurt!"

Poe had a glimpse of Chris staring down at him and then vanishing abruptly. He heard the hard pound of boot heels crossing the saloon floor, and he struggled to free himself from the table and the Yaqui's legs. Kicking clear, he rolled to his belly, his own gun now out. He threw a glance at the door. Vickery and Chris were gone, ducking into the darkness of the street.

He leaped to his feet and started for the exit. The dark shapes of three men blocked the way. It was the two saloon patrons who had earlier hurried out. They had with them now a huge, burly individual who wore a star on his faded vest.

"What the hell's goin' on here?" the lawman demanded, waving his pistol at Harper.

"Been a killing, Joe," the bartender called excitedly. "Dead and laying over there—behind that table."

Poe, stopped in his tracks by the deputy, motioned toward the street. "Those two men—the ones that went running out of here—you see where they went?"

The lawman eyed him coolly. "Didn't see nobody come out. Drop that gun your holdin', mister, unless you want me to put a slug in your belly. You won't be needin' it again."

"Don't be a fool!" Harper snapped. "I'm not looking to kill anybody. I'm trying to——"

"You ain't tryin' to do nothin' but set a spell in jail till the marshal gets back. Now, drop that gun!"

Harper rocked back on his heels in disgust. He allowed his weapon to fall. It struck the bare floor with a loud clatter. He stared at the big deputy.

"What do you mean—set in jail? I shot in self-defense. Dead man's name is Wyatt. He's an outlaw. He pulled down on me first. Ask the bartender."

"You can do your explainin' to the marshal. He'll be back, come mornin'."

"Morning!" Harper echoed in helpless rage. "I can't hang around here until then! By that time that pair I'm after can be in the next county!"

"You're dead set on gunnin' them, too, ain't you? Won't hurt none, havin' you cool off for a few hours. What you so set on killin' them for?"

"He was stirring up a fight, Joe," one of the patrons volunteered. "Came walking in here, all tough and mean like, trying his best to make them draw——"

"That's a lie—and you know it!" Poe shouted, whirling on the man.

"Lie? You saying you didn't come in here honing for trouble?"

"Not for trouble. I was looking for them."

"Same thing—leastwise, ended up that way," the deputy observed. "Why you chasin' them?"

Poe Harper hesitated, considered his answer. It could be a mistake to tell the deputy his reasons. Bringing the law on the United States side of the border in on a matter that concerned Mexico could stir up a vast amount of complication—complication that would consume time he could not afford to lose.

68

Luis Salcedo would never understand the delay.

"Personal matter," he said, finally. "No sense telling you about it."

"Suit yourself," the deputy replied. "Maybe in the mornin' you'll change your mind."

"Doubt it," Poe said wearily. He turned to the bartender. "Don't be leaving town. You're my witness."

The man nodded soberly. "Sure. Like you said, he shot first. Be glad to tell the marshal all about it."

Harper made one more desperate try. He glanced at the deputy. "Hear that? Ought to be all the proof you need. No sense in holding me all night."

The lawman wagged his head stubbornly. "Reckon we'd still better wait for the marshal."

Poe glared at the man, and then quite suddenly he was too tired to argue. There was no use fighting it. He could do nothing but wait out the absent marshal—while Chris and Hart Vickery again slipped from his grasp.

"All right," he said heavily. "Where's your jail?"

The deputy leaned down, scooped up Harper's pistol, and thrust it under his belt. He motioned at the door. "Just start walkin'. It's across the street, down a couple of doors. And don't try nothin' cute or I'll blow your backbone clean through your belly. Understand?"

Harper said nothing, simply moved for the exit. At that moment he remembered Rojo Peralta. He glanced over his shoulder, intending to tell the Yaqui to care for the horses and, if possible, find out in which direction Chris and Vickery had gone. Surprise flooded through him.

Peralta had disappeared.

ELEVEN

AS THE IRON GRATING OF THE LORDSBURG JAIL CELL slammed behind him, renewed anger exploded within Poe Harper. He spun to the deputy.

"This is a hell of a way to treat a man! What was I supposed to do—stand there and let that bastard shoot me down?"

The big lawman only grunted, turned the lock, and walked heavily into the adjoining office. There was a clatter as he tossed the ring of keys onto a table.

"Have to wait till mornin' afore you can eat. Ain't nobody open this time o' night."

"Forget it!" Harper snarled, and threw himself onto the edge of the bench that served as a cot.

He was too upset to care much about anything. While he stalled through the hours waiting for the marshal to arrive, Chris and Vickery were making good their escape. They would be far away by the time he could again take up their trail. Worse, they knew he was after them; now they would be doubly cautious.

He squirmed about on the hard seat and swore deeply. He had a good picture of what he was up against. He had wondered how Chris would react when he learned what the score on Muleshoe was, but he needed to speculate no longer. Chris was no different from the other outlaws. He wasn't about to give up that gold for the sake of the ranch—or anything else.

Harper tried to find it in his heart to not blame him too much; after all, he would be giving up not only a small fortune, but his life as well. The Mexican authorities were out to stop the depredations of *bandidos norteamericanos,* and the men who had

70

robbed the Sabine mine and killed four guards in the process were going to be a prime example of south-of-the-border justice. They would show no mercy to any of them.

He'd know how to figure Chris the next time they met, however; he would handle him just the same as he would Vickery—as a dangerous outlaw deserving no quarter. Maybe he was wrong to consider his brother in such light, but Chris sure as hell wasn't acting like a brother. He guessed he hadn't been far wrong in his attitude toward Chris. It was Rojo who was off the track there.

What the devil had happened to the Yaqui?

One minute he was in the saloon, the next he was gone. It was too much to hope that he had followed Chris and Hart Vickery—not when you considered how he felt about the matter. But where had he gone? Had he simply pulled out, refusing to give any further aid in a situation he believed was wrong? It didn't sound like Rojo Peralta—but in the past couple of days the Yaqui had changed.

It was stuffy in the small jail. Harper blinked his eyes hard and shook his head. The need for sleep was pressing hard. He swung about and stretched out full length on the bench. It was like a slab of granite, but he was too tired to really care. Up front he heard a chair scrape across the floor. The huge shape of the deputy filled the connecting doorway, hung there for a moment, then vanished. Poe heard the light click of the front door closing as the lawman went into the street.

Harper rose, stepped to the grating, and quietly tried the lock. He knew in advance that it was secure, but he had to test it. The bars rattled but remained firm. He grunted, turned back to the bench, and again laid out his lean length. Staring at the ceiling he thought of Edwina, of Luis Salcedo, of what he would do if this night in jail cost him Chris and Vickery and, resultingly, Muleshoe. Goddamn lousy two-bit lawman! The fat deputy's pigheadedness could mean just that—losing everything he owned, ever hoped to have. If he—

"*Patrón . . .*"

Only half-awake, Poe Harper sat bolt upright. He glanced about the cell, frowning. He was not sure if he had been dreaming or had actually heard the Yaqui's low voice.

"*Patrón—la ventana . . .*"

Harper sprang to his feet, no doubt in his mind now. He crossed to the barred window high in the wall. He dragged the bench over and stood upon it. His head was then on a level with the small square of bars.

"Here," he said. "Thought maybe you'd run out on me."

"No, señor. I did not wish for the marshal to take me also."

"Glad you made it. Any chance of getting me out of here?"

"*Impossible.* The fat one sits in a chair at the front door. I cannot pass by him. But there is news of Chris and the other I would tell."

Harper's interest kindled. He drew nearer the window. "What kind of news?"

"They have gone east—for Las Cruces. Already they ride."

"Cruces!" Poe echoed in despair. "And I've got to squat here in this stinking jail all night waiting for that marshal to show up." He paused. "You sure of it?"

"*Sí, Patrón.* I go to the stable to take the horses. There I learn of this. I leave your bay and ride east

72

myself for a time. I see two men. It is Chris and the other."

"You didn't try to stop them, of course," Poe said, his tone faintly derisive.

"This I could not do. They were far."

"Oh, sure," Harper said, anger and frustration turning him short-tempered and unreasonable.

Las Cruces . . . it was a hundred miles distant—and their heading for that tiny settlement made sense. They couldn't go south into Mexico—and they wouldn't try for Tucson again, not with Juh and his bloody savages prowling the hills in between. They could go north. It was a shorter ride to the nearest town, Silver City, and it would be the natural route for them to take.

Harper's thoughts halted. Likely that's what they wanted him to think; they figured he would assume they had struck out for the nearest town of size—so they chose the opposite. But they had slipped up; they hadn't planned on Rojo Peralta being free and keeping tabs on them.

"There is no doubt, *Patrón,*" Peralta said from the darkness outside the window, mistaking Harper's reason for a lengthy silence. "In this thing I cannot agree with you, but I would not lie."

"I'm not doubting you," Poe said. "Was just thinking about it. Lucky for me you spotted them. I'd have probably headed for Silver City, figuring they went that way."

There was no sense, of course, in sending Rojo to trail them. It would be a useless chore, accomplish nothing. He would have to follow anyway, and time was slipping by fast. More days would be lost now while he trailed the two men deeper into New Mexico—and God only knew to where else.

"Rojo," he said, coming to a decision, "I want you to go back to Muleshoe."

"To the ranch?" the Yaqui exclaimed in surprise. "How can I be of help to you if I return? . . ."

"Only way you can help. Hard to say how long it will take me to catch up with Chris and that bastard he's siding. If I'm lucky and they hole up in Cruces, it'll still mean better than a week lost—getting there and getting back. And they may not stop. They may keep on going now that they know I'm trailing them."

"It is true also that El Paso is not far from Las Cruces—matter of few miles."

"They won't go that way. Wish they would, but they'll stay clear of the border. My hunch is they'll head out across Texas, try to reach Kansas. Or they could go on up the Rio Grande Valley and keep right on moving until they get to Montana or Wyoming. That would put them about as far from Mexico as they could get."

"It would be well thought."

"Best thing you can do is go back to the ranch. Tell Salcedo what's happened—that four of the outlaws are dead. Tell him I'm running down the others and that they have the gold—"

"Aieee—that accursed gold!" the Yaqui moaned softly. "It will mean death for many before this ends. I feel it so. Already many lie dead."

"Tell him I'll bring them and the gold in as soon as I can," Poe continued after the interruption, "but that I've got to have more time."

Peralta made no comment. Poe realized the Yaqui was again thinking of Chris, of one brother willfully causing the death of another. Impatience ripped through him.

74

"What the hell's the matter?" he demanded harshly. "You still feeling sorry for Chris?"

Peralta's soft, liquid tones came through the bars. "When the moment comes, *Patrón,* this thing I do not think you can do."

"The devil I can't! You just watch me!"

"A brother is a brother. And blood runs thick—and strong."

"Forget it! Chris sure isn't thinking that way, so there's no reason why I should. You saw how he acted there in that saloon. When it comes down to that gold or me losing Muleshoe, he picks the gold. You hear what I said to tell Salcedo—that I need more time?"

"*Sí, Patrón.* I hear. I will tell him."

"Make him understand. Make him see that it will take more time."

"That I will do. *Adiós, Patrón. Vaya con Dios.*"

"*Adiós,*" Harper replied, but he did not know if the Yaqui was still there and had heard him or not.

He remained for a time by the window, breathing in the sweet night air, staring at the velvet-black star-studded sky. His thoughts were again of Edwina, of Muleshoe, and then, inevitably, they swung full circle and settled once again on Hart Vickery and Chris.

What would their plans be? They would rush to leave the immediate area, of course. They would do their best to throw him off their trail, now that they were aware of his intentions; they would also know that he would not remain long in Lordsburg, that he would be freed from jail after a short time.

He got down off the bench and tried to put himself in their position. What course would he follow if he were endeavoring to elude pursuit? Ride into Texas? Head for the Indian Nations—for Kansas?

He decided he would do none of those. Communications were better established in that part of the country. Texas had been a state of the Union for a good many years, and the law-enforcement agencies were many and efficient. Crossing the breadth of Texas would be risky.

He would choose to head up the Rio Grande Valley. New Mexico was a territory, only under American domination for about twenty-five years. It was still sparsely settled and with scarcely any law organization. It would be simple to drop out of sight in that rugged country, just as it would be easy to remain well hidden in the towering mountain fastness of Colorado on to the north.

And once beyond Colorado he could stop worrying about being caught. Mexico would be miles away, and the persons encountered in the Northern states and territories wouldn't care what had taken place below that distant border.

That would be the way he would do it if he had to make a choice. And if he could be certain Chris and Hart Vickery thought along the same lines, he could save time by slicing across country and intersecting the Valley somewhere above Las Cruces, possibly around Socorro. Such would put him ahead of them. But he could not be sure.

He did not know how well either of the men knew the area. Chris, he recalled, had been through there once or twice on cattle drives in the days before he broke away from the ranch and went his own way. After that his wanderings were a mystery. And Vickery . . . He could be a stranger to the territory or a well-versed native. It was impossible to know.

Poe Harper shrugged wearily and brushed it all from

his mind. There were too many sides, too many possibilities to be considered. Best to play it straight and simply follow the outlaws and not try outguessing them. He could end up outsmarting himself.

He lay back on the bench and stared through the window. Still full dark. He groaned. It would be hours before the marshal showed up.

TWELVE

THE MARSHAL'S NAME WAS HERNDEEN. HE WAS AN old man, well into his sixties, and he wore his white hair to shoulder length. He had watery blue eyes, a trailing mustache, and a sun-leathered face. He sat back in his chair and, from behind a littered table that served as a desk, surveyed Poe Harper. Dust particles floated aimlessly about in a shaft of morning sunlight streaming through the window to his left.

"I've heard of you. Heard of your pa, too. You got a ranch down in Mexico—Chihuahua State. Your pa's dead now. I'm told you're quite the *gran caballero* down that way."

Poe said nothing. He had made no explanation of the Wyatt shooting other than that the outlaw had made the first move. It seemed the smart thing to keep his reasons for being in New Mexico to himself. But Herndeen was misinterpreting, was assuming that Poe's silence indicated an unwillingness to deal with small-town authority.

"I'm asking you again, Harper, why you're in Lordsburg and what that killing was about."

"Had somethin' to do with a lot of gold, Marshal," the beefy deputy, heavy-eyed for want of sleep, said.

77

"I'm asking him," Herndeen said.

Poe, impatient with the senseless delay, clung to his rising temper. "It was a personal matter. That's all I can tell you. What about it? You turning me loose?"

Herndeen sighed. "You're cleared of the shooting. Bartender backed your story. Who was them two other men? Where'd they go?"

Poe remained silent and simply stared at the old lawman. Herndeen drummed on the table. His fingernails, yellowed with age, were curved, hooked, looked more like steer horns than something of human origin.

"You be looking for them? I take it this thing ain't over."

"Far from it," Poe snapped. "You finished?"

"Simmer down now, Harper," the big deputy broke in angrily. "Marshal'll tell you when he's done."

"It's all right, Joe," Herndeen said. "We won't get nothing out of him. One thing," he added, leveling a gnarled finger at Poe, "I don't want no more shootings in my town—no matter who you are! You got problems, you settle them somewheres else. That clear?"

"Clear," Harper said. He reached forward, picked up his revolver, jammed it into its holster. "Far as your town's concerned, I'm damned glad to get out of it— and it's not likely I'll be back."

"Good," Herndeen said bluntly. "You pulling out right away?"

"Soon as I can get my horse."

"What I was hoping to hear."

Harper wheeled and strode from the cramped, stuffy office. He paused a moment in the early sunlight warming the street, and glanced up and down. The livery barn stood to the left, a hundred yards distant.

78

There was another farther on, at the edge of the settlement. Likely Peralta had used the nearest. He spun on his heel and walked to it rapidly, his long body taut with urgency.

The bay was in a rear stall. It had fed and rested, one beneficial byproduct of Poe's enforced stay. Harper paid the hostler and began to throw on his gear. The bay, anxious to be moving, stamped nervously as it was being prepared.

In short time Harper was in the saddle and back on the street. Remembering suddenly that Peralta had carried half their trail grub in his saddlebags, he made a hurried inspection of what remained. It was a full three days' ride through rough country to Las Cruces, and it was best he not depend on the scattered ranches and homesteaders for food.

Accordingly, he replenished his stock at one of the local stores, filled his canteen, and a half hour later rode from the settlement, swinging southeast to skirt the low-lying tail of the Burro Mountains. The day was going to be hot, he realized, when he circled the last of the crumbling rock formations and broke out onto the Antelope Plains. But it was always murderously hot on that wide, fifty-mile flat of sand, cactus, and little else.

By noon he was sucked dry by driving sun and had made far too many passes at his canteen. He began to horde its contents, aware that it would have to last until he reached the Mimbres River—and he would be fortunate to make its shallow depth by midmorning the next day.

He halted in a brushy arroyo north of the Victorios shortly after noon to rest the sweating bay and have a bite of lunch. He gave an hour to this, easing his impatience by chucking pebbles at a curious prairie dog that kept poking its round head above a burrow in the well-populated village.

He felt good when the brief layover was ended, and he mounted the bay in high spirits. The sun was not bothering him too much; life on the edge of the Chihuahua Desert had hardened him considerably to the discomforts of dry heat, and he urged the bay to a slow lope.

As he rode he racked his brain hoping to discover a way he could cut down the traveling time to Las Cruces, but he came up with nothing. He was following as direct a route as possible, and a mile was a mile regardless of how you covered it. Besides, he was pushing the bay, and horseflesh could do only so much.

He spent the night at the foot of a low bluff protected by a thick stand of saltbush and mesquite from the chill wind that sprang up at sundown. It was an uncomfortable camp, and by the time the first gray flare of dawn was lighting the sky beyond the ragged rim of the Goodsights, he was in the saddle and moving on. He was stiff and sore, and he felt burned out. A stubble of black beard covered his cheeks and chin, and a layer of tan dust had begun to change the color of his clothing to a dull sameness.

The wind blew all that day, sharp-edged with sand, and the brief stop he made at the Mimbres to refill his canteen and allow the bay to ease its thirst was only a minor break in the otherwise monotonous hours. By nightfall he had reached the Goodsights, worn, nerves whipped to raw points by the maddening wind, grimly angered at what he was being subjected to.

But he was less than a day from Cruces, and that cheered him; one day from catching up with Chris and that Goddamned bastard of a Hart Vickery. It didn't occur to Poe that he was not including his brother in the same blasphemous category as Vickery. If it had, he might have wondered if there were more truth in the words of Rojo Peralta than he liked to admit.

He had reached the point where he gave no deep thought to anything, however; his being had resolved itself into a single purpose—find Chris, Vickery, and the gold and get back to Mexico. That was life in its entirety, and there was no room for other consideration. Find Chris. Find Vickery. Get the twenty thousand dollars of Sabine gold. Return to Luis Salcedo and save Muleshoe. Do it soon. Time was running out.

He did not know if Peralta would be successful in persuading the Federale captain to extend the deadline. Salcedo had been definite. But the Yaqui would try, he could be sure of that; but the ill feeling that existed between the haughty high-born and the half-breed left much to be desired where cooperation was concerned.

He wished now he had instructed Rojo to swing off-trail, stop by McGarritys, and ask the rancher to accompany him back for a talk with Salcedo. Ed might have more influence with the officer than the Yaqui. But it hadn't occurred to him, and it was too late for wishing.

Harper was astride the weary bay again well before sunrise, anxious to reach Las Cruces well before dark. If he could hold the horse to a steady pace and cut rest periods short, he could make it. But as the blazing sun swept by overhead in its cloudless, steel-blue cloak, he saw he was making poor time.

To offset this he dropped into a system of dismounting and leading the bay instead of halting completely. In this manner he relieved the horse of his weight and afforded the animal some degree of rest. For himself, he pushed on stubbornly, relentlessly, ignoring his screaming leg muscles and aching back, the burning in his throat and eyes. He could rest later—after he had put Chris and Vickery in Salcedo's hands and Muleshoe was no longer in danger.

Sweat-soaked, his features taking on the look of a lean, hungry wolf, he rode into the village late in the afternoon. The town was no more than a dozen sagging buildings squatting in a green swale on the east bank of the Rio Grande.

He toured the short main street searching for two horses that could be those of the men he pursued—and did not find them. There was a buckboard in front of the lone saloon, a light wagon pulled up at the side of the general store. Otherwise, the wide, dusty lane was deserted.

His nerves razor sharp from despair and disappointment, he cut back to the livery stable he had earlier bypassed, and rode through the shaded entrance. A Mexican hostler roused himself and moved forward languidly. Poe dismounted, stood for a minute relieving his tightly drawn muscles, and then faced the stableman.

"Looking for two men. A redhead and an older fellow. Dark. Narrow face and small eyes. You seen them?"

The hostler yawned, stretched. "*Quien sabe?*"

Harper's anger boiled over. He seized the man by the bib of his overalls, jerked him upright, and hurled a torrent of scathing Spanish at him. The Mexican's eyes opened wide. He jerked off his battered hat hastily.

"*Sí, señor,* I see them."

"When?"

"They come last night. Very tired they were."

"Where are they now?"

"That I do not know. They have ride on."

Damn the lousy luck! Poe smashed a fist into the palm of his open hand. He was too late. He would have to keep going, keep trailing, searching—and it all added up to more lost time, more delay. His frustration fading into an acceptance of a fact, he turned again to the hostler.

"They rode on—which direction?"

"To the north. Up the river."

Harper swore anew. He had guessed right. Had he been gambler enough to accept his hunch and angle across the flats to Socorro, he would have been in position to intercept them; but he had ruled against it. Now there was nothing left to do but follow.

He passed the reins of the bay to the Mexican. "Give him some grain and a little water. Rub him down. Do a good job and there's an extra dollar in it for you, *compadre*. I'll be back in a couple of hours."

The hostler grinned. Harper wheeled slowly and returned to the street and the afternoon sunlight. A couple of hours. He and the bay needed a hell of a lot more rest than that, but he had to keep moving.

THIRTEEN

POE HARPER HALTED IN AN ISLAND OF SHADE CAST BY a small cottonwood at the corner of a churchyard. He was so beat that he could scarcely put one foot before the other to perform the mechanics of walking. His red-rimmed eyes moved along the few buildings, then settled on the dust-marked window of the saloon, and his interest quickened.

A couple of stiff drinks—that's what he needed. And then some food. Together, they should whip him back

83

into feeling halfway human. His tongue came out, and licking his dry, cracked lips, he crossed the street and entered the low-roofed building, which was being patronized at that moment by three men.

It was cool inside the adobe-walled structure, and a solitary, sooted lamp hanging above the plank counter shed a weak yellow glow over the small room, adding little to the light filtering in through the window. The customers turned to stare at Harper appraisingly as he came in. He brushed aside their curiosity with a head-on, hostile glance and took his place at the end of the bar.

"Whiskey," he said in a voice ragged from the heat and dust. "Like something to eat, too, if you've got it."

The bartender placed a glass and a half-empty bottle before him. "Can give you some chili and beans, maybe a little sidemeat."

"Do fine," Joe said, filling his glass to the brim. "Make it in a hurry."

The bartender's thick brows lifted. "Figured you for just riding in. What's the rush?"

"Pulling out right away," Harper said, and raised the glass to his lips.

The raw, fiery liquor hit him a solid wallop. He gagged briefly, then refilled the shot tumbler. The bartender moved off to get the food. Farther along the counter the three patrons again considered Poe with interest. One, an old man dressed in the coarse homespun of a farmer, grinned in friendly fashion.

"You look like a pilgrim that's just found out it can be a long piece between saloons."

Harper nodded, said, "That's me," and let it drop. He was in no mood for light conversation.

"Come in from the west?" the homesteader continued.

84

"Lordsburg."

The man whistled softly. "Hell of a ride across them plains. And them mountains ain't no daisy picking."

Poe began to feel the effects of the whiskey. His muscles loosened slowly. Some of the ache was leaving his bones, and a comforting laxness had begun to seep into his body. Taking the bottle and glass, he pulled away from the counter and settled himself at one of the tables placed against the wall. He downed his third drink and leaned back. Moments later the bartender reappeared, carrying a plate of food in one hand, a small granite coffeepot and a tin cup in the other.

"Figured you'd be needing this," he said, indicating the pot as he unloaded it all on the table.

"You figured right," Harper said, and immediately began to eat. The bartender filled the cup with steaming black liquid, then reached for the bottle of whiskey.

"Leave it," Poe said. "Not finished yet."

The man wiped his hands on his apron, moved back behind the bar, and took up the chore of polishing glasses. The farmer had resumed conversation with his friends, their voices a low, running sound in the quiet. A wagon rolled by in the street, its iron tires grating against the sand, and over in the church a woman sang, practicing a hymn for the sabbath services.

Harper ate steadily, hungrily, his body and temperament warming to the soothing influence of food and drink as the moments passed. Finished quickly, he pushed his plate away. Immediately the bartender came over.

"You must've needed that. Want another go at it?"

"Got enough," Poe replied. He pointed at the bottle. "Get yourself a glass and have a drink with me."

The man studied him warily. "Sort of had you spotted

as a man with troubles," he said. "Well, I ain't seen nobody, and I ain't heard nothing. Fact is, I'm plain dumber'n hell . . . Now, if the offer still stands . . ."

"It does," Harper answered, managing a grin. "All I'm interested in is the quickest and best way to get to Socorro."

The bartender provided himself with a glass and sat down. He helped himself from the bottle, then said, "Quickest and best—means two different things."

He sampled the liquor, placed the glass on the table, and hunched forward on his elbows. "Best way is by the main road. Follows the river. Everybody uses it. Quickest is by the old Jornada. Man can save a whole day if he's willing to try it."

The Jornada . . . Jornada del Muerto—the Journey of Death, literally. Poe had heard of it, but only vaguely. It began somewhere north of Las Cruces, around Fort Selden, he thought, then laid a straight, burning path across ninety miles of hell to the outskirts of Socorro. Early Spanish explorers had followed it and given it the name by which it was known. Only a fool, it was said, would take that road. A fool—or a man hard-pressed and in one hell of a hurry.

Well, he was in a hell of a hurry—and maybe he was a fool, too, but that didn't matter. By saving a day he could overcome the lead Chris and Vickery had gained on him.

"Been told it's a mean trail," he said, pouring himself a second cup of coffee. He had consumed enough liquor. It was making him lightheaded.

"Mean ain't the word for it," the bartender said, wagging his head. "It's a son of a bitch seven ways from Saturday. But, like I said, it's a day shorter to Socorro, and if a man's in a powerful rush . . ."

"It can be crossed."

"Right. Takes guts and a good horse. And plenty of water. You won't find no spring—not between the start and the finish."

"Could be what I'm looking for," Poe said. "Got to catch up with a couple of friends there. How do I—"

"You really aimin' to ride the Jornada?" the farmer broke in unexpectedly. Harper had not been aware that the old man was listening.

"Some reason why I shouldn't?" he asked, his tone a bit sharp.

"Reason? Plenty of reasons! Man's *loco* to try it any time, but right now—August, fellow'd have to be plumb crazy! You'd be fried stiff before you got through the second day. You better stick to the main road, friend."

Poe shrugged and ignored the man. He reached into his pocket and glanced across at the bartender. "How much I owe you?"

"Dollar and a half'll do," the man said, rising. "If you decide to take the Jornada, won't be hard to find. Just head north from town, and you'll run smack into it. River curves to the west. You keep going straight."

The farmer leaned back against the bar, his head wobbling unsteadily. There was a dazed look in his eyes, not entirely due to the liquor he had drunk; he was finding it difficult to believe what he had heard.

"Man's sure got to want to see Socorro bad to foller the Jornada," he declared. "He sure does."

Poe got to his feet and winked at the bartender. "Obliged to you. Straight north, you said."

"Right. When you see the fort, that's the beginning. You'll find yourself riding between two mountain ranges. The San Andreas will be on your right, the Caballos to your left. Things start going bad for you,

87

just remember the Rio Grande is behind the Caballos, so head that way. There's another fort out there—Fort Craig. You won't see it till you're fairly close to Socorro, however."

Harper nodded again and started for the door. He felt much better, from either the food or the whiskey, he wasn't sure which. Halfway out, the farmer's voice caught him.

"Boy, you sure better do your traveling at night, if you're taking the Jornada. I'm telling you as a friend. It'll double your chances of getting through."

Poe said, "Thanks," and continued on. He stepped out into the hot sunlight and turned toward the general store. He needed no groceries, but he'd need an extra canteen. He purchased the container and walked on to the livery stable.

The bay, much improved after its meal and rubdown, whinnied quietly as Poe moved into the stall. Harper patted the big horse affectionately for a few moments, then, taking his other canteen, returned to the water trough he had noticed out front. The hostler appeared at that moment, his face wearing an expectant expression.

Harper paid him off, not forgetting the extra dollar promised, and filling the containers from the pump, he dropped back to the bay. He could have saved a few minutes by having the stableman throw on his gear while he was otherwise occupied, but he preferred doing the job himself. A horse crippled by a careless job of saddling—a fold in the blanket, a chafing girth—was something he could not risk. He felt better seeing to it himself.

He worked swiftly and efficiently, encouraged by his talk with the bartender. If he could slice a day off the trip to Socorro, he could arrive there ahead of Chris and

Hart Vickery, or at least at about the same time. With luck, he would be waiting for them.

This time they would not slip through his fingers; this time he would take no chances. He would disarm, hogtie, and take them back as prisoners. This time, by God, he was going to bring the chase to an end! The two weeks allotted him by Salcedo would be about up, possibly have passed by the time he could get back to Muleshoe. But it wouldn't overrun by more than a day or two. Salcedo shouldn't object to that—not to a couple of days. If he did, Poe decided, he'd make a trip to Chihuahua City and appeal to the Governor. Likely he would be reasonable.

The bay at last ready, Harper stepped to the saddle and headed up the runway for the door. The hostler lounged against a corner post, a grin on his dark face.

"How far to Fort Selden?" Poe asked, pausing.

The Mexican cocked his head to the side. "Ten, maybe twelve miles, señor."

Harper smiled and rode out into the softening glare of the lowering sun. He would travel to the edge of the Jornada and there halt, to wait until night set in. Then he would start this "Journey of Death," as they termed it.

It could hardly be as bad as they said.

FOURTEEN

POE HARPER HALTED SHORTLY BEFORE SUNDOWN IN A brushy pocket of land a mile or so east of the fort. He was at the lower edge of the Jornada, and the heat drifting in from its seared expanse was noticeable long before he reached the point where he had decided to await night's arrival.

He had no set plan for covering the ninety miles that lay ahead; he knew only that the terrible journey had to be undertaken if he were to catch up with Chris and Vickery and return them to Mexico in time to save his holdings. Perhaps the Jornada was pure hell, and all that people said it was—but it would be worth the danger and hardship if a day could be recovered.

After loosening the bay's gear, he lay back on the warm sand and watched the sun sink into a blaze of yellows behind the Goodsights. For a time the sky was a long band of varying golds, and then it began to deepen. Slowly it dissolved into a rose, which, in turn, became diverse shades of purple that extended in lengthy strata from north to south, the darkest clinging to the horizon, the palest stretching well up into the diminishing blue of the sky.

When at last all color had disappeared and only a lead gray declining rapidly to black had claimed the west, Harper rose, made ready the bay, mounted, and rode out of the depression onto the broad, flat surface of the plain.

Faint sounds were emanating from the fort; low thuds, an occasional shout, and once he heard the clear, sweet notes of a bugle floating on the air currents. A short time later a breeze sprang up, stirring the thick folds of heat that still gripped the land. On the whole it was not too unpleasant.

The reports of the Jornada's savagery could have been exaggerated, he told himself, stifling the vague apprehension that persisted in his mind. After all, he was no stranger to the rigors of a desert; he had grown up on the rim of the Chihuahua. Anyway, it was that extra day gained that counted.

The night darkened as clouds swept in from the east,

and for a time he had hopes of a shower. But the clouds passed on, and the black overlaying arch cleared abruptly. A cold light from the stars spread across the land, covering it with a brittle silver radiance, and everything became ghostly, unreal.

Cholla cactus took on the aspect of contorted nether-beings. Small, round clumps of creosote bush altered their normal yellow cast to one of eerily beautiful gold. The long-reaching silence was oppressive, and when a sphinx moth, large as his open hand, darted from a tangle of paperflowers and brushed Harper's cheek in its erratic flight, he jerked sharply to one side.

He swore, grinned into the night, muttered, "Skittish as a spooked bronc," and rode on.

He looked ahead, attempting to orient himself by locating the two mountain ranges between which he would pass. The San Andreas to his right were easily visible, but the Caballos were not in sight. Evidently there were still a considerable distance away. Small, intervening formations blocked his view meanwhile, but he bore in mind that as long as he held to the San Andreas he could not go wrong. Eventually the Caballos would appear, and then he would be on the Jornada proper.

The Rio Grande, distinguishable by its dark, winding trail of trees and other lush growth, was fading subtly into the west with each passing mile. The stream curved away, he recalled the bartender saying, and soon he would lose sight of it and not look upon it again until he approached Socorro. It was not comforting to know that quickly now he would be miles from water in a land so vicious that the lack of it meant death in a matter of hours. But he had two full canteens; they should get him and the bay through safely.

The big horse held up well despite the long day behind him. The meal of grain, the rubdown by the hostler in Cruces, and the sporadic rests had done him much good. Several times the horse broke impulsively from a trot into a strong lope. On each occasion Poe pulled him down. Too many difficult miles lay ahead for the horse to expend its strength on unnecessary speed.

As the night wore on the wind increased its velocity. Gradually it became colder. Harper pulled free his woolen jacket and drew it on. He noted the progressive thinning of brush and other stunted growth, and by the time the Caballos thrust their irregular shape into view on his left, the flat had changed to desert in its most desolate form. Only the hardy chollas, the creosotes, and a splash of white-and-pink-flowered jimson were now to be noted.

Finally parallel with the Caballos, he halted to rest the bay. The wind had risen to a point where it now scooped sand and whirled it along with stinging ferocity. The temperature continued to drop.

Shortly he pressed on, alternately riding and resting until at last the heavens beyond the San Andreas range became a dull gray, turned then to purest pearl, and finally burst, like a gigantic flower, into a fan of golden petals.

He stopped beside the knee-high wall of a sandy arroyo and ate a quick breakfast of cold meat and biscuits. He was chilled to the marrow, but there was no wood for a fire, and he contented himself by thinking that the sun soon would be out and he would have more heat than he bargained for.

It proved worse than that.

By midmorning the Jornada was a breathless,

seething cauldron of invisible flame. Harper stripped himself to hat, shirt, pants, and boots, and began to take frequent pulls at the canteens. The sky was a brilliant mirror of steel reflecting each degree of the sun's intensity. Even the chollas appeared to droop.

There was no sign of life in the charged air or on the burning sand. Heat hung in quivering layers over the universe as far as his smarting eyes could see, and by noon he was exhausted—and ready to admit that the things he had been told about the terrible Jornada del Muerto were as true as death was certain for the unwary.

He traveled most of the day at a painful, pitifully slow pace. He was barely conscious of night's arrival; he simply met it with wooden detachment, his haggard face covered by a fine alkali dust, his eyes bloodshot and swollen, his skin stiff from dried sweat.

He rested until midnight, knowing that he had the process of intelligent passage through the withered wasteland reversed. He should have moved entirely at night and lain low during the blistering day. But it had not been possible to schedule it in that manner; he had reached Las Cruces at an inopportune hour.

He emptied the first canteen near dawn of the second morning, holding open the mouth of the half-wild bay and pouring its contents down the beast's parched throat. The horse came first in the scheme of staying alive; he must, at all costs, see that the bay did not falter and give out. A man caught in the center of the Jornada on foot was as good as dead.

The second day was a duplication of the first—the endless, sweltering miles of glittering, blinding sand; the dancing heat; the small, starved gray-green patches of half-alive weeds; the gaunt chollas forever lifting

93

their crooked arms heavenward as though begging for relief.

He moved in a flaming dream, doggedly, determinedly, grimly. The world was savagely unreal, and mercifully, his sensibilities were too anesthetized by the paralyzing, deadly heat to comprehend fully that through which he passed. It was as if hell had erupted, lay flat and bald upon the earth—and he was crossing it.

Too exhausted to follow the pattern of continual travel, he spent most of that night in the lee of a ragged black lava flow, grateful for the opportunity to escape the harsh blast of the ceaseless wind. The rest did him much good, and he awoke before daylight, his mind clearer, although he was stiff and sore from the constant battle with the merciless elements.

But the bay had wilted steadily and surely since the close of the first day. Poe spent an hour going over the horse, rubbing it down with a coarse woolen shirt he found in his saddlebags, cleaning out its eyes and nostrils with a wet cloth.

Feed was the pressing need, and Harper cursed himself for not having had the foresight to provide a small sack of grain for the bay instead of relying on the grass he expected to find along the way. On the Jornada there was no grass—only sparse clumps of a thin, dry weed that the horse cropped greedily but that did him no good.

He sought to calculate his position. He needed to arrive at some idea as to how far from Socorro he was at that moment. Time and distance had flowed into a confused nightmare of interrupted motion since he left Fort Selden, and he was not certain of anything except that he still lived—and was somewhere on the limitless expanse of the Jornada.

But the San Andreas had dwindled to low foothills, and that meant something. He scoured his mind and finally recalled that Socorro was not too distant from the termination of that sprawling range. There should be another formation lifting up behind it now—the Oscuras, he thought they were called. If so, then Socorro would be less than a day's ride.

Convinced that he had done all he could for the bay, he climbed to a point on the jagged surface of the lava bed where he could look out over the desert, and turned his gaze to the north. A ghostly white alkali sink laid an irregular pattern on the brown, baked land just ahead. Beyond it he could see the faint, blue-shadowed shape of slopes rising to a series of peaks and ridges.

Harper's pulse quickened as the gradually increasing light brought the mountains into more distinct focus. It had to be the Oscuras! Relief and exultation flowed through him. He was finally drawing near the end of the terrible journey. Grinning, he moved back across the volcanic scar to where the bay waited.

He mounted at once and moved off, almost eagerly, now angling his course slightly westward toward the Rio Grande. The river would lie somewhere beyond the hills to his left.

By the middle of the morning the killing heat and the stabbing lances of the sun were turning him even more directly toward the stream, and the thought of reaching it and the cool green band of trees and willows that lined its banks filled him with a compelling force. He was near enough to Socorro now, he reasoned. He could afford to retreat to the beckoning comfort of the river and forsake the savage Jornada shortcut for the balance of the way.

Surely he had overtaken, or at least pulled abreast of, the outlaws by that hour. His mind began to play tricks on him. Twice he thought he saw the two men, thought he watched the surprise and fear on their faces when they beheld him standing in the dark shadows along the road, waiting. But it was all in his soaring, anxious imagination.

The bay stumbled, almost fell. Poe left the saddle and began to lead the worn horse. The heat of the sand, as before, quickly burned through the soles of his boots, drilled into his feet and his legs. It reached upward until it touched his thighs and finally began to simmer in his belly. He became sick, and several times he gagged and vomited. But he kept on. He must—he could not quit. Everything depended on his getting through—on his finding Chris and Vickery.

He saw a coyote when he halted to eat a bite of lunch and rest—a thin, starved brute that gave him a hurried, yellow-eyed glance and loped on across the searing sand toward the river.

The Rio Grande must not be far, he concluded a few minutes later after his dulled, slow-acting brain had digested that bit of information. The coyote would not try living on the Jornada. Nothing save a few whiptail lizards had caught his attention since that night near the fort.

Encouraged by that thought, he mounted the bay and pressed on. Two hours later, his eyes puffed and almost shut from the punishing glare, his body sweltering under a coating of dust and sweat, he broke from a narrow wash and saw the fresh green of trees in the distance.

He opened his cracked, bleeding lips, and a croaking sound came from his throat. He halted, took a small drink from his canteen, poured the reminder down the exhausted bay with generous abandon. He had made it! In another half hour there would be plenty of water. And shade. And coolness. And he would escape from the pitiless sun.

It took almost an hour. The bay, once it got wind of the river, found new strength somewhere in its thick body and lurched into an ungainly, trembling lope. The animal reached the river, plunged off the low bank into the knee-deep water, halted, dropped its head.

Poe Harper fell from the saddle and went full-length into the silty current. He lay there, arms outflung, legs apart, and allowed the water to wash past him. He rolled over, rolled back, luxuriating in the cool wetness as though endeavoring to soak the scorch of the sun forever from his body.

Finally, some time later, he pulled himself dripping from the stream. He was tired almost to the point of collapse, but the water had brought to him a mild restoration of his powers. Taking up the reins of the bay, he led the horse to the opposite bank. Reaching there, he paused to look back toward the east; he hoped the day would never come when he again would be forced to dare the Jornada. Once in a man's life was enough.

He rested in the shade while the bay gathered in huge mouthfuls of the lush grass growing thick along the river, and then he swung to the saddle. The main road that led to Socorro would be on ahead, he judged; probably a hundred yards or so. It should be easy to locate.

He saw the worn, beaten paths left by countless wagon wheels almost immediately. A fresh surge of satisfaction rolled through him. He had no way of knowing if Chris and Vickery had already gone by; he would have to move on into the settlement, look about, and make inquiries. But one thing was certain; he was near them—either just ahead or just behind. The shortcut across the Jornada had placed him in that position.

That thought had just passed through Poe Harper's mind, when the bay shuddered suddenly. The sharp crack of a rifle reached him in that identical instant. The big horse rocked to one side as its legs folded beneath it.

Harper tried to throw himself clear. His right spur caught briefly against the saddle skirt, delaying him. In the next moment he was down, under the bay.

FIFTEEN

HARPER'S HEAD STRUCK THE SOLID, UNYIELDING EARTH a sharp blow. Lights popped before his tortured eyes, and a gray fog passed through his mind. Pain stabbed cruelly up his left leg and settled in his knee as the bay's weight crushed upon it.

He lay motionless, shocked, unable to move. The thought *Ambush!* fought its way through the mist clouding his brain and registered dully. Apaches! His faculties began to function as the possibility of the fierce warriors being close by drove home. He struggled wildly, trying to pull his leg from beneath the bay. He moved an inch, perhaps two, but the accompanying pain was excruciating.

He lay back, breathless. Somewhat calmer, he began to reason. It couldn't be Apaches this near Socorro. Then who? The answer came like a sudden, vivid flash of lightning—Chris and Vickery! It had to be them. Who else would have cause to ambush him?

They had probably spotted him when he came to the

river. A horse and rider would have loomed large on the long, barren slope in the bright sunlight. They had then pulled off into the brush and watched him approach, ease his dryness in the river, and then move toward the road. One of them had taken a shot at him, hopeful of ending the pursuit once and for all. By sheer luck the bay had flung up its head at the exact moment and had taken the bullet in its brain.

Poe remained quiet, knowing he had likely hit upon the exact truth. Curiously, what occupied his mind in that wholly quiet measure of time was the question of who had fired the bullet. Had it been Vickery, or had it been Chris? Probably Vickery, he decided, and then felt a disturbing doubt creep into that conviction. Why couldn't it have been Chris? Being brothers meant nothing to Chris. He had made that clear. Why wouldn't Chris do all possible to protect his life along with his share of the Sabine gold?

Apparently they believed him dead and now were riding on, secure in the knowledge that they no longer need fear being trailed. A gust of anger rushed through Harper. He was a hell of a long way from being dead! And now that all the cards were out on the table and he knew exactly where he stood with Chris, the devil and all his brimstone wasn't going to stop him!

He began to struggle anew to free his imprisoned leg, clenching his teeth and ignoring the frightful pain. That no bones were broken he was fairly sure, thanks to the tough wood of the hickory stirrup that was also trapped under the horse. It supported a considerable portion of the bay's ponderous weight. He felt his leg move another inch . . . Encouraged, he dashed the sweat from his forehead and worked harder.

Abruptly, he froze and became absolutely quiet. His

ears had picked up the slow, soft beat of a horse walking upon the packed humus floor of the grove. A branch swished. Leather creaked. Eyelids squeezed to slits, Poe watched and waited.

A sorrel horse appeared through the brush, the white blaze on the bridge of his nose showing up in sharp relief, then the neck, the front quarters—and finally a man. Harper's jaw tightened. It was Hart Vickery. He was hunched forward, alert, his narrow-set eyes swinging back and forth. His glance settled on Poe's sprawled shape. His head came up. He halted the sorrel and eased back in the saddle.

A chill traveled up Harper's spine as the outlaw's bleak gaze raked him. Vickery probably figured he was not dead, only stunned and unconscious from the fall. He would finish the job now. Poe, partly hidden by the bay's body, allowed his hand to ease to the pistol on his hip. At that moment he saw Vickery tip his own revolver upward and hook his thumb over the hammer. The three distinct clicks of the weapon being cocked were loud in the stillness.

Harper's fingers wrapped themselves about his .45 and drew it soundlessly from the holster. Masked by the bay's bulging belly, he worked it into firing position. He watched Vickery lower his pistol, level it, take aim.

Poe jerked to one side and triggered two fast shots over the bay's bulk. Simultaneously, smoke blossomed in the outlaw's hand. Quick, searing fire slashed Harper's head. He recoiled, knew he had been hit. He lay there numb but alive, wondering.

He moved his head, relieved that he could. Immediately he remembered Vickery and cocked his pistol for a third shot. It wasn't necessary. The outlaw was folding slowly over his saddle, arms dangling loose

100

at his sides, legs stiff and out of the stirrups. The sorrel began to shy, unaccustomed to the odd position of its rider. The movement displaced Vickery. He fell to the ground.

Pain began to throb in Harper's head. He lay back again, breathing fast, eyes on the fading wisps of smoke drifting off into the brush. After a moment he raised his hand and with the tips of his fingers explored the stinging wetness along the side of his head above his ear. A tough grin pulled down the corners of his lips.

"Son of a bitch damn near got me," he muttered aloud. If the bullet had been a quarter of an inch to the left, he would have had no more problems to face.

Pain wrenched him in a sudden wave. He lowered his head to the spongy ground, easing it. Something stirred in the grove, and his hand tightened about the smooth handle of his pistol. But it was a single sound, and he did not hear it again; an animal of some sort, he reckoned. He raised his head once more and peered over the bay at Vickery, who was sprawled face down, one arm oddly upheld, caught in the stiff, upright branches of a snakeweed bush. He had not stirred.

Harper relaxed while a flood of anger and frustration had its rough way with him. Five men dead now—two by his own hand—and he was no nearer his goal. There must be something to the curse of the Sabine gold. It was jinxed—*oro del maldito,* as the Yaqui had put it. Everyone coming in contact with it met with bad luck—or ended up dead.

And where was Chris? He must have been somewhere close when Vickery fired his first shot—and the second. Was he back in the shadows now, biding his time for a chance to finish what his outlaw pal had started?

Regardless, Poe had to get out from under the bay. He began to work feverishly at the chore, impatiently pulling and tugging at his leg while pain lashed at him with sickening force. The weight of the bay pinned him securely to the ground. Finally he gave it up, gasping for wind and near exhaustion.

He lay there seeking to reason out the problem. He had managed, through all his frantic efforts, to move his leg no more than three or four inches. At the rate he was going he would never get loose—and he could die before anyone happened along.

He drew himself to one elbow and looked around. His glance fell upon a short length of wood, a limb about the thickness of his arm torn by the wind from one of the broad spreading cottonwoods. If he could get it, use it as a pry . . . He threw himself back full length, arms outstretched.

The sudden violent motion sent pain screaming up his leg, throbbing through his head. He set his jaw and extended his right arm to its fullest. His fingers touched the limb. Twisting his wrist, he clawed at the wood with his nails, felt it move . . . Moments later he was able to grasp it. A sigh slipped from his lips as he pulled it to him.

He forced the length of wood under the bay, running it alongside his leg until it touched the heel of his boot. Then, praying that the limb would not snap, he pried upward. The bay's belly gave. Poe felt the pressure go off his knee. He doubled his leg, groaning at the pain, and jerked himself clear.

Exhausted from the exertion, he sat for a time breathing deeply and then got to his feet. His leg buckled immediately, throwing him to the ground as fresh pain burst through him. The knee was badly bruised, and there could be some torn ligaments. He could expect plenty of trouble for a few days; still, he guessed he should be glad no bones were broken.

He straightened up, favoring the injured member, and hobbled to where Hart Vickery lay. The outlaw had died instantly. One of the bullets had caught him in the left breast, the other a bit lower. Poe Harper sagged against the trunk of a nearby cottonwood, again sick while the now-familiar feeling of frustration raged through him. How many more would die before he completed the chore that faced him? How many?

Maybe Chris was already dead. Maybe that was why Vickery was there in the grove alone. If so, he would have all the gold with him. Poe turned hastily—too hastily—and went half-down as his knee failed. Pulling himself up, he limped to where Vickery's sorrel waited.

Working hurriedly, he unbuckled the straps of the bulging saddlebags and thrust his hand into the bellowed depths of one of them. Beneath several items of clothing he could feel the bars of gold—small, one-inch-square, six-inch-long rectangles. Each had been wrapped to prevent its clinking. He replaced the buckles and examined the opposite pouch. It contained a similar amount. There wasn't twenty thousand dollars' worth there—about half that, he estimated. It meant Chris was still alive and possessed the remainder.

He secured the pouch, moved to the head of the sorrel, and taking up the reins, led the horse into the open. Halting, he glanced down at the bay. A twinge passed through him. The big horse had been a fine mount, one that had not let him down. It was a hell of a note that the beast should make it across the Jornada, and then die just when the worst was over.

103

He wished he could claim his own saddle. He had used it for years, but he knew he would never get it off the dead bay. He would have to be satisfied with Vickery's gear—as well as his horse. Vickery wouldn't mind, he thought grimly as he knelt and began to remove the items he wished to keep from his own saddlebags. Where Vickery had gone, he'd have no use for a horse.

He should do something about the outlaw's body. It was wrong to leave it there in the grove. And the killing should be reported to the law in Socorro. Harper groaned at that. Such would mean more delay, as in Lordsburg—and this time he had no witness to back his story. The hell with it, he decided. He was too close to finding Chris to get sidetracked now. He'd handle it another way.

He dug around in his pockets for the stub of pencil he always carried. Then, taking one of the blank bank drafts from his saddlebags, he laborously wrote a note.

Sheriff of Socorro:

This outlaw, name of Hart Vickery, killed my
horse. Tried to kill me. I killed him instead. If
you need to talk about it, find me at the Muleshoe
Ranch, Chihuahua State, Mexico.

Resptfly.
P. Harper

He returned to Vickery's body, affixed the note to a button on the man's shirt, and then mounted the sorrel. He wouldn't rely on someone stumbling across the body; he would drop word that a dead man was lying along the south road when he reached Socorro.

That would send a half a dozen or more riders pounding off to see who it was and what it was all about.

He didn't mind facing the law for what he had done; he had made it plain in the note that he was available. It was simply that he could not spare the time. Later, after things were cleared up with Salcedo and life was back to normal, he'd make the trip to Socorro and answer any questions the law might wish to ask.

Chris was the important consideration now. He must find him, catch him before he got away again. The logical place to look first was in Socorro.

SIXTEEN

HE RODE INTO THE SETTLEMENT FROM THE SOUTH, loping the sorrel down a long hill that ended at the shaded plaza around which the town was built. Pulling up to one of the several hitchracks, he halted and dismounted, aware of curious glances from many of the persons moving along the board sidewalks.

Securing the sorrel, Harper stood for a time hopefully scanning the horses waiting at the rails. Chris was riding a white-stockinged bay, the mount he had always considered his own and had taken when he left Muleshoe. The big, handsome gelding was not on the street.

Poe grunted wearily. Nothing ever came easy, it seemed. Now he would have to look inside every saloon and whorehouse in town. Dog tired, he turned and angled across the dusty street to the first bar. It was deserted. He glanced to the Roman numerals on a clock hanging on the wall above the mirror and glassware.

Four-fifteen. Too late for the day trade, too early for the evening.

He returned to the sidewalk, checked out the next two saloons in quick order. There were a few patrons in each; and all stared at him, frankly curious; but Chris was not among them.

He came to the corner, wondering if it would not be smart to turn his attention to the livery barns. If Chris thought him dead, he would probably decide to spend the night, possibly several days and nights, in the town. Socorro would be to his liking; it was known as a good place insofar as women and gambling were concerned. The bay would be in a stall, if he had made that decision.

Harper sought out the largest stable, entered its cool, familiar-smelling interior, and walked the length of the runway, peering into each narrow compartment. He reached the end but saw nothing of the bay. He was about to retrace his steps; when he drew to an abrupt halt. Chris's horse was standing in a corral at the rear of the building.

Pulse quickening, he crossed to the yard and took a closer look at the horse, anxious to be sure. It was the bay. The brand of Muleshoe stood out plain on his left hip.

"Mighty fine bit of horseflesh," a voice said unexpectedly from behind.

Harper whirled, startled. The stablekeeper, an elderly man with iron-gray hair and a heavily seamed face, fell back a step.

"Didn't figure to scare you," he, said hesitantly. He stared at Poe, eyes fastened to a place above his left ear.

Harper managed a grin, realizing then that the man was looking at the bloody track left by Hart Vickery's

106

bullet. He had neglected to clean it off. It was what had taken the attention of others along the street and in the saloons.

He brushed at the slight wound. "Got myself raked good, coming through some brush."

The stable owner smiled. "Ought to be putting something on it. Liniment, maybe." He paused and pointed to the bay. "Seen you admiring the gelding. Fine horse."

"For a fact," Poe said.

The man moved in eagerly. "I'm Rafe Carr—own this here place," he said, extending his hand. "You looking to make a good trade?"

Surprise ran through Poe. That Chris would sell the bay was hardly believable. Why? He certainly would not be in need of money.

"Man sure would have to be in a bad way to sell a horse like that. He yours?"

"Is now. Traded for him this afternoon."

Harper nodded. "Think I know the gelding—and the man who owned him. He around somewhere?"

Carr shook his head. "Rode off west—in a powerful hurry. That's how come he was in a trading mood. Said he needed a fresh horse—and a fast one. The bay here was about played out—but that's all that's wrong with him," he added hurriedly. "Needs graining up and a couple days' rest. Then he'll be in A-number-one shape."

Poe was only half-listening. Chris had known of the shooting, had figured him as well as Hart Vickery for dead. He had decided to get the hell out of the country before anyone connected him with the killings. But why had he gone west? That made no sense. Why would he change directions?

"You sure of the way he went?"

"Hell yes," Carr replied firmly. "Seen him line out myself. Even asked me how far it was to Magdalena."

"Red-headed man—grins a lot?"

"That's him. Why, you looking for him?"

Harper shrugged. "Let's just say I know him."

He backed away from the corral, no longer interested in the bay. He wanted to get back on the saddle and move on. He was tired, but Chris would not be far ahead now. Suddenly he remembered Hart Vickery's body.

"What was that killing south of town?" he asked casually.

Carr came to attention. "Killing? What killing? Never heard nothing about it."

"Well, there was one," Poe said, moving slowly toward the stables. "Some big-time outlaw, I think. Heard talk there was a party riding down there for a look. About ten miles."

The lie came easily. Poe winced inwardly as it passed his lips, then eased his conscience by telling himself it was only a small lie—and for good purpose. He didn't want to think of the outlaw's body lying out in the brush for the coyotes and buzzards to quarrel over.

"Expect I ought to be looking into it," Carr said. "I'm kind of on the coroner's jury, most of the time." He glanced at Harper. "Reckon you ain't interested in the bay, eh?"

"Not today. You go ahead. Maybe I'll drop by later."

"Obliged to you," the livery man said with a relieved smile. He wheeled and broke into a trot.

Poe returned to where he had left the sorrel and eyed it critically. The horse appeared to be in excellent condition, and it was evident that Vickery and Chris had taken it easy coming up from Las Cruces. Why then had

Chris traded off the bay? Both horses had covered the same ground, should be equally fresh or worn. Something had gone wrong with the bay, he concluded. Probably had turned up lame. It was the only possible answer—and since Chris wanted to get out of the country fast, he sacrificed his favorite horse in the interest of haste.

But Chris could not get away fast enough or go far enough, Poe thought as he swung to the saddle. He was only a few hours ahead, and he was riding across an area with which Poe was familiar. He had made several cattle drives over the long flats and by the towering mountains that laced the land. No matter which way Chris turned, Poe would know exactly where he planned to go. Chris would have been smarter to continue on northward.

Poe circled the plaza and veered into the narrow street that led to the road west. He glanced at the sun, hanging above the lead-colored ridges and peaks of the Socorro Mountains. Still a couple of hours until sunset. Magdalena was a good twenty-five miles distant. It would be dark by the time he reached the mining settlement, named for the saint whose face some fancied they saw in a rock formation at one end of the towering range.

Chris would be needing rest, Poe realized as the sorrel began the lengthy grade lifting from the flat along the river where the town squatted. He might consider it safe to stop and spend the night in Magdalena. Harper sighed, hoping he was right; he was so weary that he could scarcely stay upright on the saddle. His knee pained steadily, sullenly, and there had been no letup of the throbbing in his head.

It seemed weeks, rather than days, since he had

enjoyed a night's sleep. Muleshoe and its comforts were far away, couched in a remote corner of his mind, seemingly almost a dream of what had once been. And Edwina—he wondered about her, what she was doing at that moment, and if she thought of him. Did she know he had left Mexico and was on a grim hunt for outlaws who threatened the future they both looked forward to? Was she aware that he stood to lose everything if he failed in the task that had been forced upon him?

And Rojo Peralta—how had he made out with Salcedo? The two-week deadline was about gone— would be by many days before he could now return with Chris and the gold . . . That damned gold! That lousy, bad-luck gold. The stories were true; it did have a curse on it.

Five men dead—plus the four guards slain in the holdup. And God only knew how many more had died digging it out of the mountains, smelting it, pouring it into the oddly small ingots and getting it ready for the politicos. It wasn't over yet, either. There was no way of knowing how Chris, without his partners, would react now when the showdown came. Poe hoped it would not end in gunplay.

Paradoxically, he could contemplate taking his brother in and handing him over to Luis Salcedo for certain execution—yet he rebelled at the thought of having to shoot it out, possibly killing Chris himself. Somehow, there was a difference.

It was ironic that it had dwindled down to Chris and him. Why couldn't the last man in the chain have been one of the others? Why couldn't it have been Chris instead of Tom Schrader killed in Skeleton Canyon by the Apaches? It would have made it a hell of a lot simpler all around.

Poe Harper shrugged, finding himself deeply disturbed by such thoughts. He was thinking about his own brother, his own blood, in a way no man should.

He stirred angrily. Why shouldn't he? Why not look upon Chris in the same light as he considered Vickery and Wyatt and the other outlaws? Chris had demonstrated that family ties meant nothing to him; he had compelled Poe to place him in the same category of all outlaws. It hadn't been Poe's choice.

Harper's head came up suddenly. A scatter of yellow lights in a pocket of the dark, cloud-shrouded mountains lay below. Magdalena. The sorrel had made fine time—and Poe had been so wound up in his troubled thinking that he had not noticed the miles, had failed even to note the setting of the sun.

Rousing himself from his abyss of weariness, he rode into the brawling, noisy little settlement, crowded with miners and prospectors, card sharps and saloon girls, and halted before the first bar he came to. He had misgivings as to the gold packed in his saddlebags; he doubted the wisdom of leaving it unattended on the horse while he made the rounds of the saloons and makeshift hotels. But it would not be smart or even practical to take it with him.

His glance fell upon a man standing slightly out of the pushing, shouting crush that clogged the main street. The man watched him with steady interest. A match flared in the hand of a passerby, and its flame glinted upon the star pinned to the man's vest. Harper grinned. It was a bit of good luck—a quick answer to his problem.

Favoring his injured knee and leading the sorrel, he limped to where the lawman leaned against a porch-roof support.

"Evening," he said. "Busy night."

The town marshal considered him dourly and nodded.

"Looking for a friend of mine. Was told he headed this way."

The lawman jerked his thumb at the surging throng. "Help yourself," he grunted.

Three men, arms linked for mutual support, reeled by, all laughing and talking. One rolled his head back, grinned in slack-faced friendliness, and shouted, "Come on, Marshal—join the shindig. Down at Hooten's place!"

The lawman's impersonal glance followed the trio until they were swallowed by the swirling crowd and thick dust, then pivoted back to Harper.

"Your friend got a name?"

"Harper. Chris Harper."

"Never heard of him. What kind of a horse was he riding?"

Poe remembered he had not asked Carr, in Socorro, what Chris had traded for. He shifted his weight, fighting the leaden weights that dragged at him, and said, "Don't rightly know, but he's a big fellow. Red hair. Usually grinning."

The lawman bobbed his head. "You didn't miss him much," he began, then stopped as six shots, fired in rapid succession from somewhere near the center of town, sounded flatly above the racket. He listened for a few moments, finally added, "Was here couple, three hours ago. About dark. Kept going."

Harper's hopes sagged. "Already been here," he muttered, more to himself than the lawman. He looked up, eyes heavy, glazed with fatigue. "Any idea where he was going?`

The marshal pointed at the road. "Silver City, I reckon. Was the way he took out."

SEVENTEEN

SILVER CITY . . .

Despair settled over Poe Harper. Silver City was three days' steady riding—actually nearer four. And with the lead Chris had there was no possibility of overtaking him before he reached there.

He felt the lawman's eyes drilling into him, hard, unfriendly. That he had his hands full looking after his town was apparent; that he wanted no more strangers moving in to cause him further worry was also evident.

"You figure to stop over?"

Poe looked out over the street, over the broiling crowd restlessly flowing to and fro in a noisy, boisterous current. A woman laughed shrilly. Somewhere glass shattered and a man swore wildly. He shook his head.

"Good thing," the marshal said gruffly. "Town's full up. Got yahoos sleeping in the street. One hell of a mess."

"Everybody's got problems," Harper said, and turned away. Too beat to lead the sorrel through the pushing, shoving throng, he went to the saddle. Walking the big red slowly, he made his way back to the road, ignoring the angry glances, the sharp words hurled at him from those shouldered aside by the horse.

He reached the main trail that ran westward across the San Augustine Plains, and he halted there at the fringe of the settlement to stare vacantly over the endless, rolling flats glowing softly beneath the light of the moon and countless stars. Coyotes yelped in the low hills, and off to his left in the dual rows of rundown shacks that sagged one against the other along Whiskey Alley, a dog barked in a spiritless, monotonous fashion.

113

The sorrel shied nervously, half-dancing, fighting the bit. He was anxious to be on the move. It was cool, almost sharp on the high plateau where Magdalena nestled, and the red felt good. Hart Vickery had been an excellent judge of horses, if little else. The sorrel had been on the go all day and that evening and was still full of fire.

Without conscious thought Poe Harper relaxed the pressure on the leathers and touched the horse with his spurs lightly. The sorrel leaped away and began to lope down the long grade. Poe settled into the saddle. The knowledge that four more days on the trail faced him was discouraging; but Chris had struck out for Silver City, and he could do nothing but follow.

A wooden man with a wooden mind, he kept at it until the sorrel tired. Then, in a small canyon gashed on the west side of the Magdalenas, he halted and made camp. Too exhausted to prepare a meal, he simply munched disinterestedly at the rock-hard biscuits and paper-dry sliced beef from the supply in his saddlebags, washing it down with water.

He realized, as he dug about in the leather pouches, that he had left most of his food stores in the saddlebags on the luckless bay. He should have made a replacement in Socorro or Magdalena, but his slow-functioning mind had not thought of it. Still, he'd make it. He was too worn to worry about it.

When the first gray filled the sky beyond the mountains to the east, he rose and brewed himself a lard tin of strong coffee. He wanted nothing else, and he moved on after he had drunk his fill.

He allowed the sorrel to pick his own pace, a long, easy lope, and he covered the miles effortlessly. The heat increased as the sun climbed higher, but it was not too bad on the San Augustines. The altitude was considerably higher than that of the Rio Grande Valley, the Jornada, and the land to the south, and the temperature, while hot during that period of the year, in no way touched the one hundred degrees plus through which he passed in that area.

When Horse Mountain, a solitary eruption of tree-covered slopes rising out of the plain, came into view, Poe began to alter his westward course and veer more to the south. To continue on the main road would throw him far north; it was wiser to strike across open country and thus save several hours of riding.

He wondered if Chris had remembered to do likewise, and a small hope lifted within him when he realized that his brother likely was not well enough acquainted with the country to take the more direct route. Heartened by the thought, he held the sorrel to a lope across the rolling, cedar-studded, grass-covered hills; he might just cut Chris's lead by an hour or so after all.

The subsequent days and nights flowed by with repetitious, unvarying monotony. He rode, he stopped, he ate and rested—and rode on. He was three and a half days making the trip, and when he swung into the end of Silver City's narrow street and stared vacuously at its false-fronted buildings perched high above the sidewalks, its slant-roofed houses clinging to the slopes of the crowding hills, he was as a man in a trance, devoid of sensation, of reaction.

So worn and unmindful was he that when he learned from a stableman that Chris had been there, paused briefly, and pushed on for Tucson, he simply accepted the information with a nod of his head and continued along the road. To his fagged brain the pursuit of his brother had evolved into a way of life; he had been at it since the beginning of time, it seemed. And he would continue until the end, he thought grimly.

He replenished his short stock of supplies at a general store near the edge of town, rousing himself sufficiently to ask a few questions. No, the proprietor had not noticed a red-haired man pointing west—but then there were quite a few riders coming and going. He could have missed seeing him, particularly if he had not stopped to make a purchase.

Yes, it was the only road to Tucson. Due west until you reached Duncan, a town right on the New Mexico-Arizona line. Then angle southwest, skirting the upper end of the Peloncillos. You went on through the Pinaleno Range, the Galiuros, and finally the Catalinas. Tucson lay on the other side of them. How far? One hundred and seventy-five miles—and every mother's son of them was there.

Poe Harper departed the settlement and halted in a pine grove a few miles beyond its outskirts where a small spring put forth a thin stream of water to shape a shallow pond. While the sorrel grazed on the purple seeding grass and took his fill from the sink, Poe tried to collect and organize his thoughts.

Salcedo's deadline was up. It had run out sometime during the leg from Magdalena to Silver City—he was not certain exactly when, for the days since he had first ridden out of Muleshoe with Rojo Peralta on what he thought was to be a brief trip were now little more than a blur.

That did not mean, however, that he could slacken the pursuit; Salcedo, if he had granted his request for additional time, would not have agreed to more than a week's extension. And now that could prove too little,

116

even if he found Chris in Tucson and started immediately for Mexico. But he could come close if everything went right, once he had Chris in tow.

Chris, he was sure, would not pass on through Tucson. The town held some special attraction for him—a particular woman preferred above all others, perhaps. Or it could be for a different reason; possibly it had to do with the gold.

Tucson was a terminal point for smugglers, had been for many years. There were men there who could handle the ingots for Chris, convert them into cash money. Possibly that was why the town had been the outlaws' original destination and was again that of his brother. Yes, Chris would be there—and the end would then be in sight. He could only hope that it would not come too late to save Muleshoe.

He rested until dark and pushed on, beginning once more a succession of days and nights that blended into a lengthy tedium of lonely hours. From the coolness of the high country, he sank gradually into the steadily warming deserts of Arizona. The hills changed, some red, some green, some gray; they fell off to plains marked by cactus, an occasional filmy smoke tree, countless clumps of saltbush and creosote bushes, lifted again to towering bluffs and ragged mountains that glistened in the sunlight.

The sorrel plodded on tirelessly. Day . . . night . . . boundless stretches of sand, glittering hot under the sun, eerily beautiful with ghostly saguaros beneath the moon.

He killed a mountain lion in the deep shadows of the Pinalenos as it tried to get at the red. Vultures, soaring in ever-shrinking circles, caught his lagging attention south of the Galiuros, and he had a time of fear and uncertainty, wondering if the great winged scavengers

117

could be hovering over Chris, down and helpless because of an accident. But they were too far south, he finally decided, and forgot them.

He saw a party of Indians—Apaches, he was sure—just after he crossed the San Pedro River. Taking no chances he sweated out two hours in a blistering brush pocket until they had disappeared into a trailing cloud of gray dust. Later, when night overtook him at the edge of the Catalinas, he made camp, denying himself a fire, which would have provided much-needed coffee, because of the Indians. There could be others skulking about.

Dog tired, he stretched out on his blanket to rest. He bore little physical resemblance to the Poe Harper who had ridden out of Mexico almost three weeks before. An inch of ragged black beard clothed his jaws. His face had leaned to a sun- and wind-tortured, leathery triangle; his eyes had taken on a quality of fierceness and looked out upon the world with a sullen hostility.

He limped noticeably from his bruised knee, and the mark of Hart Vickery's bullet had scabbed over and healed and now was a white, hairless line carving a trail above his ear. His clothing had faded, worn thin and converted to the color of dust. His boots were scarred by brush and knife-edged rocks, the heels broken and turned under. Only the dogged, relentless determination of the original man had remained constant and unchanged.

He rose early the next morning, mounted, and traveled steadily. He entered the scatter of low-roofed adobe huts of Tucson late in the afternoon, with the sun streaming down from a cloudless sky, and headed for the center of the sleepy, age-old settlement.

As he turned the last corner and faced the row of

business houses, he pulled up short. Three men stood in the shade afforded by the roof of a saloon porch, not twenty feet away.

One of the three was Chris.

EIGHTEEN

POE HARPER STARED.

He was stunned by the unexpected confrontation. He thought of the days and nights, the endless miles, the hardship, the deprivation, the violence and sudden death; and then to turn a corner and abruptly come face to face with the reason for it all was a shock. It bordered on the wryly humorous.

Chris had apparently been in Tucson long enough to clean up, shave, and put on fresh clothing. Poe saw him start involuntarily when his casual, drifting glance paused on Vickery's sorrel, then stiffen to rigidity as his eyes lifted and beheld the grim figure of his brother.

Poe grinned, a hard core of exultation gripping him. The long fingers of his weather-toughened hand dropped to the butt of his pistol. His eyes, glittering, hardened visibly. He would not lose Chris this time.

Chris saw the overt motion. His head came up slightly. He said something to his companions. Both half-turned, gave Poe a brief look, then moved off down the sidewalk. From the tail of his eye Poe watched them, sharp and suspicious. As they continued on Chris came off the boards slowly, deliberately, taking each step with care. A half dozen paces away he halted.

"Poe . . ." he began hesitantly, his voice strained. "I—I thought you were dead . . . Back there in—"

"Not quite," Harper said harshly. "You and your

119

partner damn near got me. You missed by a couple of hairs."

Sweat stood out on Chris Harper's face in large patches that glistened in the driving sunlight. His brow was pulled to tight furrows, and the muscles of his face worked nervously.

"Wasn't me who tried to kill you," he said in a falling voice. "You got to believe that, Poe. Was Vickery. Claimed he saw some Apaches tracking us. I told him to forget it, that we were close enough to town to run for it, if they jumped us. He rode back anyway—wanted to make sure, he said. I waited. A little later I heard shooting. Then when Hart didn't come back, I went to see what happened. Saw you both laying there—dead, I figured."

Poe recalled the noise he had heard in the brush after the gunshots. Perhaps it hadn't been an animal, as he had thought. It might have been Chris, who had taken one look and rushed on without bothering to make sure of anything . . . But Chris could have been right there all the time, too, standing in the background not far from Vickery.

"Maybe that's the way it was—and maybe it's just another lie," Poe said coldly. "Makes no difference now. You're through running. Where's the gold?"

Chris produced a forced smile. "Safe. It's back in my hotel room. Nobody knows I've even got any. You carrying Hart's share?"

Harper nodded. "I'm taking it all back to Mexico in the morning—and you—with it. Like as not I've lost Muleshoe by now, but I've got to try. Deadline was up days ago."

Chris raised his hand cautiously and pushed his hat to the back of his head, exposing a shock of flaming red

120

hair. "Then what do you want to go back for? If the deadline's up—why give the gold to the Mexicans? Why don't you just keep Vickery's share as a sort of payment for the ranch?"

"It all goes back," Poe said dully. "I'll talk to the Governor at Chihuahua if Salcedo insists on sticking to his time limit."

Chris Harper's face fell solemn. "And I'm going with it. You're handing me over to them too."

"You're damn right I am!" Poe flared, sweating and uncomfortable in the direct sun. "I didn't chase you all over hell for the ride!"

Chris shrugged. "They'll hang me, Poe. You know that. And I'm your own brother—your blood."

Harper's lips drew into a harsh line. "Brother— blood! You should have thought about me being your brother before you dragged me into this! This kin business has never meant anything to you before—now all of a sudden it's a big thing. Seems when the boot's on your foot, it pinches a little."

Chris looked away, his face pale under its ruddy brown coat. "Reckon I have come up pretty short."

"For a fact, but it's your own doing. You made your bed—nobody did it for you. Be man enough to lie in it."

Chris sighed. His shoulders went down. "All right, Poe. Whatever you say. What's next?"

Harper came off the sorrel. A few onlookers, all beyond hearing, had paused and were watching curiously. He flung a hard glance of disdain at them as he faced Chris.

"I'm through trusting you so I don't aim to take any chances."

"That mean you're having me locked up?"

"No. I'd be forced to do a lot of explaining and it

121

would bring in the local law. Can't afford any more delay. I'm keeping you with me—and not letting you out of my sight."

Poe hesitated, studying his brother's stilled features. "If you're thinking of making a break, forget it. You'd never pull it off."

Chris smiled in a fixed way. "You'd shoot me down?"

"You're Goddamned right I would! I've done all the chasing I intend to—and like I said, you're through running." He pointed at a building at the end of the block.

"Head for that livery stable. I want to see to the sorrel. And we'll be needing a pack horse. Carrying us and the gold, too, is too big a load for two horses. After that we go to your room. I've got to clean up, get some sleep."

Chris wheeled and moved off through the ankle-deep dust toward the barn. His customary jauntiness had returned. He gave Poe a sidelong look and grinned.

"Was just thinking, going to be quite a chore for you, sleeping and keeping an eye on me at the same time, like you're planning."

Poe said, "I'll manage. Keep walking."

"You'll manage—how?"

Harper only grunted. They reached the livery barn and entered. Once off the street Poe moved up close to Chris and relieved him of his pistol.

"Didn't want to do that out there," he said. "Could cause a commotion."

The hostler materialized from the depths of the bulky structure. Poe gave detailed instructions for the care of the sorrel as he removed his saddlebags and passed them to Chris to carry.

"Be pulling out early in the morning," he said to the stableman. "I'll need a pack horse and rigging. Have one ready, and I'll settle with you then."

The hostler bobbed his head and glanced at Chris. "You be leavin' too?"

"He will," Poe said. "Have his horse ready."

Chris spun angrily on his heel and headed back up the long runway. Poe followed, walking slowly and with effort. He was so weary that each step was torture. His knee throbbed in concert with his head. They reached the doorway and stepped into the street. Looking to his left Poe saw a general store. He grasped Chris's arm, turned him toward it.

"Thought you said the hotel . . ."

"Stopping here first," Harper replied as they mounted the steps leading up to the porch.

He made only a small purchase—ten feet of half-inch steel chain and two stout padlocks. Chris eyed the transaction suspiciously but made no comment. They returned to the street, crossed over to the hotel, and went inside. Chris led the way to a room in the rear. He unlocked the door and waited for Poe to enter. Harper shook his head.

"You first. I don't trust you—not as far as I can spit."

The room was dark and cool. The walls were thick adobe blocks, and to Poe Harper the wide bed loomed up as a small piece of paradise. He could have crawled into it that very instant and slept for a week. But he pushed the need aside; there was still much to be done. He watched Chris hang the saddlebags he carried over the back of a straight chair. Sinking onto the edge of the bed, he motioned to Chris.

"The gold—get it."

Chris stepped to a small closet at the end of the room.

123

He withdrew his blanket roll and tossed it onto the bed beside Poe. There was a flat, metallic clink when it struck.

"Got it inside."

Poe moved his shoulders. "Like I said, I don't trust you. Open it up."

Chris leaned over the bed and unbuckled the leather belt that held the roll together. He spread it out. The gold, each bar wrapped in squares of old cloth, lay in the center.

"Where's your saddlebags?" Poe asked.

Chris pointed to the closet.

Poe said, "Get them."

The pouches were fine black leather, handsomely tooled. Chris dropped them on the bed. Poe reached for his pair and laid them beside those of his brother's.

"Put all the bars in mine," he directed. "Stuff you take out, we'll carry in yours."

"That mean you'll be toting all the gold?"

"Getting a pack horse to do that—along with the grub we'll need. Point is, if we run into trouble, I'll have just one pair of bags to worry about, and not two."

He shifted to the chair, sat down, and watched while Chris made the transfer. He was having difficulty staying awake, and his entire body felt limp, drained, devoid of life. When the job was finished, he said, "Put them over in the corner."

Chris carried both bags across the room and deposited them. He came back around and looked at the pile of chain. "What about that? Figured it was for the gold."

"It's for you," Poe said dryly. "Stand over here, with your back turned this way."

"For me?" Chris echoed, slowly complying.

Poe said, "That's right," and taking one end of the

124

chain, he fitted it around Chris's waist and pulled it snugly into place. Laying two links together, he snapped one of the padlocks through the loops, forming a locked circle.

"On the bed," he directed.

Mumbling curses, Chris did as he was ordered. Poe drew in the slack of the chain by winding it in and out of the bedstead's iron grillwork, then secured it with the second padlock. When he was finished, Chris could move about on the bed, but there all freedom ended.

"Now you know how I figure to get some sleep and not worry about you," Poe said, stepping back.

Chris was flushed with anger. He jerked impatiently at the chain, rattling it noisily. "Hell of a note!" he said in a low, furious voice. "Chained up like a Goddamn dog—like a criminal!"

"Which is what you are," Poe said wearily. "You're not playing games, Chris. You're an outlaw—pure and plain. It's about time you realized that."

He moved away, taking Chris's blanket with him. He would have to forego the luxury of sleeping on a mattress for a while longer. Picking up one of the pillows, he made a pallet on the floor—well beyond his prisoner's reach.

He delayed lying down until he had stripped and washed himself from the china bowl and pitcher. He was too tired to shave, and his beard was so thick that it would be a job for a barber, anyway, so he let it go. He had no clean clothing; what he had brought along was back in the saddlebags on the dead bay. He rinsed the sweat and dust from his underwear and shirt, soaked his socks, and hung them near the window to dry. After that he sprawled out on his blanket, totally beat.

Chris had fallen silent, occupied by his own thoughts. Poe, lying naked, savoring for the first time in weeks the sweet joy of being cool, clean, and relaxed, stared at the smoke-stained ceiling and wondered what might be filling his brother's mind. Was it a realization of what the future held for him—the knowledge that death awaited him in Mexico?

Poe stirred restlessly, trying to clear his mind. Chris had it coming. He had bargained for that sort of a finish when he joined with Vickery and the other outlaws in a scheme to steal the Sabine gold. Brother or not, there was no sidestepping that truth. Chris now had to pay for his crimes—and he should expect to.

"What about supper?"

The incongruity of the question jarred Poe Harper, brought a wry smile to his lips. He had thought that Chris was worrying over the days to come, that he might be feeling the sharp stabs of repentance for all the grief he had caused. Instead he had been thinking of his next meal.

"Don't worry, you'll get fed," Poe assured him.

"We're pulling out in the morning?"

"First thing."

"Why not tonight? Thought you wanted to get back to that Mex soon as you could."

"At this stage of the game, one more night's not going to make much difference," Poe replied wearily. "And I'm dead on my feet. Now, shut up and let me get some sleep."

"Sure, brother, whatever you say," Chris murmured quietly.

NINETEEN

THEY RODE OUT OF TUCSON IN THE COOL, GRAY LIGHT of false dawn. There were no words between them, only a stiff reserve, one not of anger but of strained self-consciousness. Poe guessed he had never really known Chris; he had simply grown up with him. They had played together as brothers when small, and later they had worked the ranch side by side; but in reality, Chris was a stranger.

It was the awareness of this, along with a deep-seated mistrust, that prompted Poe to make further use of the padlocks and chain. He had left the circle of steel about his brother's waist and passed the remaining length through the fork of the saddle, employing the second padlock to secure it. Chris could thus shift about as he willed and dismount when necessary, but he could move only a limited distance from the buckskin he rode.

By the time they had reached the first slopes of the Catalinas, the pearl in the east had lightened and long shafts of color had begun to spear the sky, lifting the canyons from shadows and silhouetting the grotesque saguaros, as it cast a yellow glow over the cooked land.

This changed rapidly to palest lavender, to rose, more swiftly to a huge fan of salmon, and then abruptly it was sunrise and the desert became a broad, endless expanse of harsh tans and grays and ochers warming to the glowing ball climbing out of the Dragoons.

They skirted the southern tip of the Catalinas. Poe had set a direct course for the Peloncillos and the trail that led upward to Skeleton Canyon. It was the shortest

127

route, and while it would take them into country where Juh and his Chiricahuas roamed, it was still the best way to go.

The heat rose steadily, and by noon the horses had begun to slow, suffering intensely under the sweltering sun. They halted in a shallow wash for midday lunch, rested an hour, and moved on. Night overtook them just short of the San Pedro, and they continued on in darkness until they reached the banks of the shallow stream.

They made camp there, building the smallest of fires with which to boil coffee, and shielding it well in the rocks. Poe was determined to extend no invitation to the Apaches, if possible.

Poe tried several times during the meal to draw Chris into conversation, but his brother remained tight-lipped and glum through the entire evening, responding with brief answers barely sufficient to satisfy Poe's questions.

Harper finally gave it up and dozed off with the strange, uncomfortable doubt and uncertainty with which he had been visited before, during the long, quiet hours on the trail, as to whether he was right to hand Chris over to the Mexican authorities. And as before, he assured himself that it was the proper course to follow, that he had no choice.

Chris was born to hang; therefore, why should Poe's own life's work be sacrificed merely to delay, at best, that which would come eventually. It was sound reasoning, but somehow Poe Harper could not smother one small, plaguing disturbance that had become more apparent only recently.

Late the afternoon of the second day, with the grim silence yet hanging between them, and the Dragoons to their backs, they saw a large dust cloud hovering above the desert to the north. It was farther up than Juh's usual territory, but Poe knew that Apaches were inclined to range wide, and he took immediate precautions. He held the horses to a slow walk, losing time but lifting no telltale yellow boil of their own. He called a halt at the first opportune spot to make camp.

The riders, whoever they might be, were striking south, following a line that would intersect the trail Poe had selected. As he stood on the crest of a low hill, with the sun splashing a long rose band across the western horizon, he debated the wisdom of pushing on under cover of night, or simply staying put, waiting out the horsemen until they had passed.

He returned to camp, deciding it would be better to delay until morning and again locate the dust roll. He could then alter his plans to avoid the riders if need be. Moving on through the darkness they could blunder into the party with fatal results.

"Staying here until sunup," he said, making a final check of the horses. "That could be Juh and some braves. No use asking for trouble."

Chris, sprawled on the warm sand, head resting on his saddle and toying with the chain that connected him to it, stirred disinterestedly. "Can't see as it makes much difference to me. I'm a dead man anyway."

Poe, finished with his inspection, moved back to the center of the camp. He sat down in his blanket roll and drew forth two of the slim black stogies he had purchased in Tucson. Tossing one to Chris, he bit off the end of the other, thrust it between his lips, and dug about in his pockets for a match. Chris made no effort to light up his weed but simply stared at it.

"Guess I knew this would happen someday," he said

129

finally. "Just never figured it would be like this—with you all mixed up in it, I mean."

Cupping the lucifer with both hands to hide the flare, Poe lit his cigar. He inhaled, exhaled slowly, removed the stogie from his mouth, studied its tip.

"Neither did I," he said, smoke trickling from the corners of his lips. "And it's not easy—for me."

"No need for you to feel sorry. You've got plenty to lose. Everything, in fact. I've got nothing."

Chris felt like talking. A curious relief passed through Poe. Somehow it eased his own troubled mind, did something toward soothing that gnawing in his guts.

"How'd you ever get lined up with a bunch of bastards like Vickery and Schrader?"

"Just bumped into them—over Abilene way. My first time for something big like this—killings, I mean. They want me in New Mexico for a stagecoach holdup but nothing worse than that. Reason why I got out of the territory fast as I could after Vickery got shot-up. He wanted to go to Colorado. I sort of tagged along, since we were partners, more or less. After you got him, I decided I didn't want to risk it, and I cut back to Tucson."

"Wondered why you changed your mind. That holdup, you say it's the only charge against you?"

Chris nodded. "Only one. Wasn't actually in on that shooting at the Sabine mine, either. I was down at the foot of the canyon, watching out for Federales. Sort of a lookout. Schrader and the others were the ones who jumped the guards and the courier."

"Still won't let you off the hook," Poe said thoughtfully.

"Know that, but I wanted you to have the straight of

it." Chris hesitated. He stuck the cigar, still unlit, into his mouth and began to chew on it. After a moment he said, "We had some good times when we were kids, Poe, growing up on Muleshoe."

"Guess so. Too bad it couldn't have lasted."

"Just wasn't meant to be, I reckon. I was too much like Pa, always aching to move on."

"He stayed put pretty good," Poe said, vaguely angered. "Else he'd never have built Muleshoe into what it is."

"Then I guess I was worse than Pa. Anyway, here I am, headed for a hanging—or if I'm lucky, a firing squad. Hope it all doesn't come too late to save the ranch for you."

"Got me worried. Time we arrive there, I'll be two weeks, more or less, over the deadline. Sent Rojo back to tell that Federale captain—Salcedo—that I had to have more time. Don't know if he agreed or not."

"Probably didn't. You know how a Federale soldado thinks. Besides, I got a hunch they want the ranch—that they'd like to run all the *gringos* back across the border. This Sabine Mine thing came along just right to make it all look good."

Poe frowned. "That just a hunch, or have you got some reason to believe it's that way?"

Chris shrugged. "Just sort of adds up—and I don't trust them like you do. Muleshoe would make a fine army post, and they need one in that part of the country. The *bandidos* and the *rebeldes* are giving them hell all through Sonora and Chihuahua."

Poe Harper digested that slowly. After a bit he shook his head. "Could be, but if they try it, they've got a fight on their hands—if I've still got something to fight for. I'll go clear to the head man in Mexico City. That land

131

was given to Pa. Maybe I don't have a deed, but there's bound to be a few still around who'll remember the deal."

Chris smiled wanly and reached for his blanket. "Luck," he said, "but you're putting a hell of a lot more faith in those Mex politicos than I would."

The dust cloud still hung in the eastern sky when they moved out that next morning. Apparently the riders had also halted for the night and were now resuming their journey. They seemed only a short distance farther south than they had been that previous sundown.

Around noon a new roll of tan showed up to the southwest, and alarm began to tighten within Poe Harper. They were now between two parties—both of which could be Apaches. He forsook the pattern of slow travel wherein he avoided raising a curtain of their own, and hurried on.

Immediately the cloud to the southwest altered and began to shift due east. Whoever it was had changed course, was moving swiftly to cut them off. Poe increased the pace. It was a losing battle. And then when he was on the verge of cutting away, of finding a place where he and Chris could make a fight of it, he caught sight of the approaching riders and saw it was a cavalry patrol. Relieved, he called a halt and waited for the army men to arrive.

The lieutenant in command, a bearded oldster with an erect bearing, pulled to a stop and threw a half-hearted salute to the Harpers.

"Thought you might be Apaches," he said, and added, "Lieutenant Dodge. Fifth Cavalry stationed at Camp Crittenden."

Poe nodded. "Glad to see you, Lieutenant. I'm Poe Harper . . . My brother, Chris."

132

Dodge acknowledged the introduction. When his eyes touched the chain about the younger Harper's middle, he frowned. "Your brother, you say?"

"Right," Poe answered, feeling somehow on the defensive. "On our way to San Luis Pass. And the border."

The cavalry officer continued to stare at the chain. "He your prisoner?"

"He is."

Disapproval tugged at Dodge's weathered features. He chewed at his lower lip as though struggling to understand such a phenomenon. One of the cavalrymen shifted on his saddle, glanced to the man opposite.

"His own brother," he said, scorn riding his voice. "Ain't that the Goddamndest thing you ever heard of?"

"What you reckon he done?"

"Hard tellin'. Makes no difference. Man just don't go draggin' in his own brother. Why, hell—"

"That'll do, Hennessey!" Dodge snapped, his face stern.

Quiet settled over the ranks. Dodge came back to Poe. "Except you know you're taking a chance riding through here. Apaches been giving us the devil for the last few months."

Harper said, "I know. Had a brush with them about three weeks ago." He pointed to the dust in the east. "You see that?"

"Was headed that way when we spotted you."

"Good. If you're agreeable, we'll ride along. Escort will be appreciated."

Dodge said dryly, "Imagine it would. I can take you as far as the Peloncillos. Patrol ends there."

Poe felt the cold, wondering eyes of the hard-bitten cavalrymen digging into him. Anger and resentment

133

welled through him, stirred his impatience. Who the hell did they think they were, passing judgment on him? They didn't know what it was all about; all they saw was a man taking his brother to somewhere—a prisoner in chains. They were shaping their conclusions from that. Well, to hell with them—all of them!

"Be a big help, Lieutenant," he said, his voice stiff. "We can move out when you're ready."

TWENTY

THEY REACHED THE PELONCILLOS LATE THAT afternoon. Dodge lifted his hand and signaled the column to halt at the foot of the trail. He faced Poe, his eyes red from the glaring sun, his skin covered by the white, powdery dust.

"Far as we go, Mr. Harper," he said, then added, "Luck on the rest of your journey."

Throughout the day Poe had watched the cloud to the east drift southwest slowly. It was far below them now, and any danger it might pose seemed negligible.

"Obliged," he said. He motioned to the yellow pall. "That'll be Juh and his bunch, all right. They're about where we saw them before—close to the Guadalupes. Camp's there."

Dodge nodded. "We'll have a look."

The officer raised his arm again. The beefy first sergeant behind him bawled a command, and the patrol swung off in a tight curve.

"Another man riding off to die," Chris said, his glance on the slender blue thread. "Juh's got him outnumbered three to one."

"Happens to all men, one form or another," Poe replied. "Anyway, Dodge strikes me as knowing what he's about."

Which is more than I can say for myself, he finished silently. During the past hours as they drew nearer the border and the jurisdiction of Mexico, the disturbance within him had grown more pronounced. The attitude of the cavalrymen, the words of Rojo Peralta, his own inner doubts had all combined to create conflict within him and give him no peace.

But he was right, dammit all! There could be no other answer—no other way. Chris, brother or not, was guilty; he must stand and take his punishment. When you bought booze, you paid the bartender. It was the way the game was played, and you lived—or died—by it.

Punishment be damned!

Who did he think he was ragging? It was Muleshoe that mattered to him—it wasn't any devotion to the law that had put him on the saddle and sent him through hell and across half the sand dunes of New Mexico and Arizona after Chris and the others! It was his own personal interest—actually greed! Why couldn't he face up to that?

"Let's go," he snapped curtly, impatient with himself and with the truths that stabbed at his conscience. "Want to get as far up that Goddamned mountain as I can before dark."

Chris favored his brother with a sidelong glance. He shrugged. "You're calling the shots," he said, and moved on.

Later they camped in a small meadow well screened by bushbriar and scrub oak from the road. There was always the possibility of Apaches, of a small hunting party, passing through the canyon, and Poe was taking no chances.

But he was restless and upset, anxious to reach the border, return to Muleshoe, and have done with it. He aroused Chris shortly after midnight, and with the aid of the moon and stars, they made the passage through the hushed, still-warm canyon. They encountered no Indians, saw only a pair of coyotes and a half-starved bobcat that hurried off down the trail ahead of them at a peculiar sidling gait.

It was full daylight when they reached a coulee just short of the border and halted for breakfast. Risking a small fire, Poe made coffee and heated up some of the dried meat and stale biscuits. He had small appetite. The sullen clawing within him persisted, it had strengthened during the night, and he was ill-tempered and brusque.

Chris, nursing his cup, watched him through shuttered eyes. At last he said, "Don't let it eat on you, brother. I've got it coming. I'm ready to face whatever's ahead."

"Doing what I have to," Poe replied. "Hate it, but I've got no other choice."

The words sounded defensive to him, and he stirred irritably. Chris leaned back lazily.

"But you ain't sure it's right—that it? Reckon turning your own kin in for execution would be a tough chore. Not sure I'd be man enough to do it."

"You never showed much regard for blood ties before," Poe said sharply.

Chris drained his cup, then stared at it. "Maybe not—but what I did was all accidental like. I didn't just start out to make trouble for you."

"But you did. If you had stopped to think before you

started, you could have figured it would turn out this way."

"Maybe so. Never was very smart—not like you, anyway . . . But one thing is bothering me—you."

Poe stared. "Me?"

Chris pulled himself upright. "You. Once you take me across that border, you've got a hell of a load on your conscience—and you're not likely to ever shake it . . . And something else—far as everybody else's concerned, you'll be a marked man—one who killed his own brother—"

"The devil with what everybody else thinks!" Poe cut in angrily.

"Be that Cain and Abel business Pa used to read us from the Bible."

"Not exactly," Poe said stiffly. "You earned what you've got coming to you."

Chris sighed and looked off toward the desert. "Comes back to that every time. Guess you're right. Man pays the fiddler once he's through jiggin'. Nothing ought to make any difference."

"Won't to me, but I guess I ought to tell you—I'm sorry about the way it's turned out."

Chris shrugged. "No need. Reckon it's all in the way a man's put together. Muleshoe's a fine place. Can't blame you for fighting for it—and a fellow needs something in this lousy, stinking life to hang on to. For some it's a woman. Others—like myself maybe—it's gold. For you I guess it's Muleshoe."

"Something counts for every man," Poe said quietly. "It could have been a fine thing if the ranch had meant something to you, too."

"Too late for that," Chris replied. "Too late in more ways than one. Here comes your *soldados* now."

TWENTY-ONE

POE HARPER ROSE SLOWLY, HIS FEATURES TAUT. HE looked to the desert. The sun was young, but already it was hot and low-hanging layers of heat were beginning to shimmer. Dark-bellied clouds gathering along the eastern and southern horizons were building steadily; likely they meant nothing, would only intensify the heat. It would be another sweltering day on the Chihuahua.

There were six men with Salcedo. A routine patrol, Harper guessed. Then he wondered—was it an accident that the Mexican officer led his cavalrymen so near the border, or was he intentionally maintaining a sharp watch? Regardless, he was there, and with him came also the moment of truth.

Silent, Poe watched the riders draw closer. They came at a lazy jog, their weapons glinting in the harsh light. When they were within fifty yards Salcedo lifted a gauntleted hand and brought the small column to a halt. He remained motionless for a long minute, his browned face toward Poe and Chris, and then he rode forward alone.

"Your move," Chris murmured softly.

Poe half-turned, stared thoughtfully at his brother for a brief time, then wheeled to the pack horse. He removed the saddlebags containing the gold, hung them over his shoulder, and again glanced at Chris.

"Wait here," he said, his face an expressionless mask, and walked on to meet Salcedo.

Chris frowned. "What do you want me . . . " he began, and let the words die as Poe shook his head.

Harper came to a halt beside the stone marker that indictated the exact line of the border. Salcedo, resplendent

138

in blue and gold, the jeweled saber glittering at his side, squared his shoulders and saluted briskly.

"*Buenos dias, señor.* It has been a long time."

Poe nodded, allowing the saddlebags to fall to the baked earth. They made a chinking sound. Motion over to his extreme right caught his eye. A lone horseman broke from the scanty brush and approached at a lope. Rojo. Apparently he, too, had been keeping close tab on the trail.

"A lot longer than I figured on," Poe said, returning Salcedo's greeting. "Everything all right at my place?"

"All is well," the captain replied. If he were impatient to get his hands on the gold and the one surviving prisoner, he made no show of it. "The mestizo is one of great efficiency. The cattle and the fields prosper."

Poe said, "Good. There been any trouble between my people and the soldiers?"

"None. My men have their orders. They obey. Bandits did come but were driven off with no damage to the property. All is well with you, I trust?"

It was the usual polite and indirect conversation favored by the Spanish and Mexican people. But it was customary, and being on uncertain ground, Poe smothered his impatience and allowed Salcedo to come to the point gradually.

"Everything's fine, Captain."

"It has been almost a full month."

"You know why I'm late. I sent Peralta to explain. Ran into trouble at the start. I've covered a thousand miles more or less since we last talked."

"It was a great inconvenience, I know. What of the criminals?"

"All dead but one. Not all my fault. The Apaches killed three. I was forced to defend myself against two."

139

Harper paused, hearing the *vaquero* move in behind him to take up a stand.

Salcedo's glance reached beyond Poe and rested on Peralta. Then, "You have proof of these deaths?"

"Proof!" Harper exploded, exasperation finally getting the best of him. "How the hell could I have proof? What did you want me to do—cut off an ear and bring it to you?"

Salcedo shrugged. Sweat, glistened on his cheeks and trickled down into the high collar imprisoning his neck in small rivulets. "Perhaps it would have been wise," he said gravely.

"Well, you'll have to take my word for it or go hunt up Juh and ask him—along with the marshal in Lordsburg and the sheriff of Socorro. Now, let's come to busines. Where do I stand? You extend that deadline?"

Salcedo removed his shako. With an embroidered handkerchief he wiped sweat from his forehead, then carefully replaced the showy headpiece.

"I did so, señor. It was my own decision. There was not time to reach the Governor." He paused, and glanced at the sky. "The sun is hot. It is best we conclude. I will have the gold and the prisoner."

Poe leaned forward, picked up the saddlebags, and tossed them to Salcedo. The officer allowed them to fall at his feet. Then with the toe of his boot he touched the bulging pouches.

"It is all there?"

"Wouldn't know," Harper said. "Never counted it. It's what they had on them, and they didn't get much chance to spend any of it."

"It is understood," Salcedo said. "And now the criminal."

In the succeeding hush Poe Harper turned and

glanced over his shoulder. Chris had not moved; he still waited with the horses. He brought his attention back to Peralta. The *vaquero's* features were set, grim. He read nothing there.

"Captain," Poe said, returning fully to Salcedo, "he's not going with you."

A small sound of relief escaped Rojo's throat. Salcedo's eyes flared with surprise, and his brows lifted. He stared at Poe.

"It was the agreement!"

"I know that, but I'm turning him over to the law in my country. He is wanted for robbery. He will go to the pen for a long time."

Salcedo stirred angrily. He raised his hand and beckoned imperiously to his men. They moved up at once.

"This I cannot permit," the officer said when the cavalrymen were lined up behind him. "He must be punished by Mexico."

"Not necessarily. New Mexico has first claim on him. The robbery charge has been standing for quite a spell. Anyway, he didn't do any of the killing at the Sabine Mine. He's guilty of being a party to the robbery but not of the murders."

"It is you who now splits hairs," Salcedo said, his swarthy face reflecting his disappointment. He was silent for a few moments; then he said, "I have able men with me. I would avoid trouble, but I am thinking of taking this man with me by force."

"Better think again," Poe said dryly. "Put one foot over the line and there'll be trouble—plenty of it. We'll fight you, and when it's done you'll have a tough time explaining spilled blood on my side of the border to your government and mine."

In the tense hush that followed Salcedo studied Harper intently. Finally he shrugged. "It is better there be no bloodshed, but it changes that which was agreed upon by us. You do not complete the terms of the arrangement. It is therefore my decision that the ranch becomes forfeit."

"Why?" Poe demanded. "You've got all you wanted. You have the gold. All the outlaws are dead except one, and he's going to jail for a long time. Seems to me your government ought to be satisfied."

"It is not as my exact orders specified—"

"The hell with your exact orders!" Harper exploded suddenly. "You've done what you were told!"

"With the gold and a prisoner—yes. It could be truly said that my duty has been discharged. The deaths of the others could be explained, perhaps proved, if need be. But while one criminal still lives . . ."

"Behind bars in a penitentiary."

"It is not the same, señor."

"Practically. By God, Salcedo—I'll go to the Governor—"

"You will not cross the border!" the officer broke in sharply. "I warn you of such. You will do so under penalty of arrest. You are considered an enemy of my country."

"Enemy!" Poe yelled, taken by surprise. "What the devil do you mean by that?"

"You have sheltered criminals, enemies of Mexico. You now protect one. Therefore you are also an enemy."

"Goddammit, Salcedo, I told you I didn't know they had done anything wrong when they stopped by my place."

"Perhaps, but you will not cross, señor," the Federale

said firmly. "My soldiers patrol this area. Others are stationed at the ranch you choose to call yours. An attempt by you will end not only in failure but in disaster for you as well. Since yours is the same name as the criminal we seek, an error could easily be arranged."

Wild words rushed to Poe Harper's lips. He pressed back the outraged flow, brushed at the sweat on his face.

"Muleshoe is mine, Captain," he said more calmly. "And so is everything on it. You're stealing it from me."

"There is no theft—"

"The hell there isn't. I've lived up to my side of the bargain—in fact, if not to the letter."

Salcedo shook his head stubbornly. Temper had also faded from him. "There is no fulfillment. It can only be accomplished by your delivering to me that man who is your prisoner. If that is done you may return in safety and unmolested to your ranch. All will be settled."

Again Poe glanced at Chris, at Rojo Peralta. He shook his head. "No deal, Captain. It's my way or else."

Salcedo sighed heavily. He motioned to the nearest soldier to pick up the gold. "As you wish, señor. I am grieved that you will lose so fine a ranch. I can see much of your heart is buried there. It is a great loss, I know."

"If you feel so damn sorry for me," Poe snapped, "how about going to the Governor and giving him the whole story? Tell him the facts. If he's an honest man, he'll agree that I've done all I could."

Salcedo looked off toward the long band of brushy hills beyond his waiting soldiers. Clouds were piling up there, too, and a faint breeze, although hot, had begun to stir.

"It is necessary that I return the gold to Chihuahua," the officer said. "I will do as you ask—

143

but I promise nothing. The Governor is a man of stern qualities—one of the military. He does not change his thoughts with ease. Meanwhile my men will patrol the border. I will not ask for your word not to cross. It is better that I simply prevent such. This is understood?"

Harper nodded slowly. "How long before I can expect to hear from you?"

"It is a journey of considerable distance. Let us say two weeks."

"What about my ranch while you're gone?"

"A few soldiers shall remain. Also"—he pointed at Peralta—"the mestizo is welcome."

Poe lowered his head and brushed at his whiskered jaws. "Guess that's the way it will have to be. I'll meet you here at the marker two weeks from today."

"Agreed," the Mexican captain said. "Now I shall go. *Adiós, señores.*"

"*Adiós,*" Harper replied, and watched the officer turn toward his horse.

TWENTY-TWO

POE STOOD IN SILENCE AS SALCEDO AND HIS MEN wheeled away. Peralta stirred at his shoulder.

"Let only a small hope dwell in your heart, *compañero*," the *vaquero* said softly. "The *ricos* are not *ricos* for no cause. I fear we shall see no more of our fine Muleshoe."

Harper nodded numbly. "Was the only thing I could do, Rojo. The only thing."

"And it is right. Content yourself with that thought. It is my great pride that in the end you had the courage to

144

cast away the curse—the evil spell of the Sabineros—and be a brave man."

Poe laughed harshly. "Damned if you haven't almost got me believing that crap!"

Peralta stared at him briefly, then shrugged. "It is of no matter now. It is finished."

Harper's shoulders slumped. A sigh slipped through his cracked lips. "You're right. Everything's gone—down a rat hole. I end up with nothing. A lifetime of work—for nothing."

"Such is not true, *compañero*. You have—"

"Let's move out," Poe interrupted wearily. "No point standing here mooning about it."

"And the rain will soon come," the *vaquero* said, turning with him.

"Be good for the range," Harper commented idly.

He swore quietly. Range—what range? He no longer owned a ranch. There was no need to worry over rain, over the grass, whether the springs would give out or the rivers run dry. Rain was just rain now, with no special meaning for him.

"Poe . . ."

He looked up at the sound of his brother's voice. Chris was standing before him, arm outstretched.

"Will you take my hand?"

Wordless, Harper reached out and enclosed his brother's fingers in his own.

"About the only way right now I can thank you for what you did. But I'm not letting it end here. I'll try and make it up to you."

"Forget it," Poe said, shaking his head.

"Not about to—ever. Guess I finally grew up and got my eyes open. I'll turn myself in to the sheriff, and when I've squared things with the law, I'll—"

Chris Harper's words checked abruptly as a distant splatter of gunshots rolled across the hot, still air. The three men whirled.

"*Bandidos!*" Peralta yelled.

There were twenty-five or thirty in the band. They swept out of the brush pockets along the Sierra Madres and bore swiftly down upon Salcedo and his small patrol. Before the Federales could turn and make a run for cover, the outlaws had engulfed them in a wave of dust, smoke, and crackling rifles.

Poe spun and took a step toward his horse. Rojo Peralta laid a hand on his arm.

"There is no use," he said. "They are too many. We could do nothing."

Harper relaxed, turning his eyes back to the desert and its violence. He had no deep feeling for Luis Salcedo, but even an enemy had a right to better odds.

"Couple more soldiers," Chris said, pointing to their right.

Two of the men left by Salcedo to patrol the border spurted from the scrubby bushes and trees, lining out at a fast gallop for the confused milling of men and horses—and certain death.

"Got guts," Chris muttered admiringly. "I'll say that for them."

There was a quick flurry of fresh gunfire as the troopers raced in. One of the men fell from his horse immediately. The other disappeared into the swirling pall.

Suddenly the desert was quiet.

The shielding cloud began to rise, drift away. Figures became more distinct. Something flashed among the horsemen now riding aimlessly about. It was the ornate saber Luis Salcedo had worn. One of the bandits had claimed it and was moping through the fallen soldiers,

146

systematically hacking their bodies, making certain there were no survivors.

Gradually, the bandits began to withdraw, leaving one upright shape, and it partly so. It was a horse sitting oddly on its hindquarters, dying slowly, dying miserably. Abruptly that bulky shadow, too, toppled.

Rojo Peralta moaned softly, his eyes on the ragged column of riders slanting for the hills. "*Oro del maldito*," he murmured. "It is always thus."

The evil gold . . . the Sabinero curse. Poe stared across the simmering flats at the dark, crumpled shapes. Seemingly it had harmed everyone who had come in contact with it. Perhaps the outlaws would have better luck.

But it had again struck at him. Luis Salcedo was dead—and the gold lost. There was no one to lay his case before the Governor—no rich ransom to bolster his plea. The last, thin thread of hope had been broken.

"Guess that wipes out Muleshoe for sure," he said in a low voice. "With Salcedo there was a chance—a slim one. Now we can forget . . ."

Poe's words trailed off. His head came up and his eyes filled with a hard brightness. "They'll likely pull the soldiers out of there now—at least for the time being," he said, only half-aloud. "If I had a dozen men—good men—I could slip down there, get my stock and the rest of what belongs to me, and get out before they knew what was happening."

Immediately Chris said, "Count me in!"

Poe wheeled to Rojo. "What about the *vaqueros?* Think they'd help?"

"They will, *compañero,*" Peralta replied. "On such you can depend."

Poe wheeled and went to the saddle. "Let's get to

147

McGarrity's," he said in a quick, anxious way. "We can do our recruiting there."

He raised his eyes, looked off across the burning Chihuahua Desert toward the south. "It'll mean the end of that Muleshoe—but there's plenty of land in New Mexico for another."

EPILOGUE

I<small>T WAS REPORTED IN</small> C<small>HIHUAHUA</small> C<small>ITY THAT A PARTY</small> of men, numbering around thirty, were drowned when trapped in an arroyo by a flash flood on the west slopes of the Sierra Madre Mountains. The men, it was said, were thought to have been bandits, but no one knew for certain. So violent was the sudden desert storm that little was left by which identification could be made.

Official Mexico took only passing note of the incident. The country could well spare thirty bandits—a hundred times that many, when you got right down to facts. It was more concerned over the loss of a brilliant young army officer, one Captain Luis Salcedo, son of a distinguished family, who met his death along with a number of his soldiers under mysterious circumstances on the desert.

There was also another matter of grave import.

A raiding party of Norteamericanos, led by a fierce, black-bearded man, had slipped down into the San Pedro River country and stolen—yes, literally stolen—an entire ranch. With the assistance of several *vaqueros* they had made off with a herd of cattle, numerous horses and wagons, household furniture—even the grain from the fields. Only empty buildings remained when they departed.

It was a grave crime and could have somber repercussions. An investigation was underway with the intentions of making formal protest to the United States Government. In the future strong measures would be taken to prevent such outrages, the Governor

149

of Chihuahua declared.

To this end it was likely an army post would soon be established at a suitable location near the border.

We hope that you enjoyed reading this
Sagebrush Large Print Western.
If you would like to read more Sagebrush titles,
ask your librarian or contact the Publishers:

United States and Canada

Thomas T. Beeler, *Publisher*
Post Office Box 659
Hampton Falls, New Hampshire 03844-0659
(800) 818-7574

United Kingdom, Eire, and
the Republic of South Africa

Isis Publishing Ltd
7 Centremead
Osney Mead
Oxford OX2 0ES England
(01865) 250333

Australia and New Zealand

Bolinda Publishing Pty. Ltd.
17 Mohr Street
Tullamarine, 3043, Victoria, Australia
(016103) 9338 0666